# ~Jim~

**By Suzann Baldwin**

## Table of Contents

A Dedication To Healing

How To Find Shaylee

What She's Doing When You Find Her

The First Chapter

Week One

Week Two

Week Three

    The Story

Week Four

Week Five

Week Six

The Next Chapter

The Last Chapter

Closure

Author's

A Letter To "Mitchell Quinn"

**Description**

**Webography**

**Special Fonts**

A Dedication To Healing

Always remember that the soul was designed
to be wounded, but still keep loving,
and the heart, to break,
but continue beating.

## How To Find Shaylee

From Portland, Oregon, drive onto the I-5 Northbound freeway. Follow it over the green steel bridge into Washington State (the "other" Washington). You'll find yourself in Vancouver, Washington (the "other" Vancouver). One of this town's charms? Its southern border is the Columbia River Gorge. Continue ahead. Past the Vancouver exits, the first few county exits, past the Clark County Events Center exit. The next town is Battleground, named for a battle that never took place.

You might notice the word city isn't being used, because Southwest Washington was settled more than built. Small groups of people harvested the thick, wild forests. Lands were cleared. Houses began to dot the landscape. Crops were planted in rich, volcanic soil. Then came schools, butcher shops, hardware stores, markets, restaurants. This area developed building by building, need by need, dream by dream.

Keep going. Now we're driving by the exit for the town of Ridgefield. The name might sound familiar because it's the birthplace of U-Haul ®. Just ahead is La Center. From the eighteen-seventies through the early nineteen hundreds, its river, the Lewis, was the "center" of commerce for the area. Any boat traveling up or down the Lewis River during that time stopped at the La Center docks. Take that exit. At the traffic circle, bear right. Head east until you come to a bridge. The old docks are gone, but look down and you can still see the remains of some of the pier posts in the water.

Pass the card rooms and the bakery. Let Pacific Highway lead you out of town. Take the next right at the horse pasture and follow the road until it disappears into the hills. To your left, you'll see a river rock driveway leading to the top of one of those hills, up to the home of Shaylee Simon. At the end of her driveway is where a story begins.

## What She's Doing When You Find Her

Shaylee stared at her phone for a long time after the call ended. James Vincent. James Vincent. International star, multiple-award-winning actor James Vincent, had just called her. James Vincent. Talented, accomplished, handsome, James Vincent.

He loved her writing, he said. Could he fly out to meet with her next week, he asked. He'd just wrapped up the sixth season of his reality show, "People Watching," and learned it was being canceled, he went on. He had an independent film project lined up, but couldn't go into any details, he apologized. He wanted an "as-told-to" autobiography released before the movie came out, he explained. He was going to have some time off over the summer, before going to Europe. Would she be available to work with him, he wondered? Six weeks, say, from the beginning of August through the middle of September?

Shaylee had no idea the turn her life would take, when, four years earlier, she'd self-published "Some Of Me." The collection of short works got immediate attention. Rumors of a new talent passed from one person to another, quietly at first, then louder and more insistent. Hints of enthusiasm grew to statements of praise. Critics noticed. Publishers considered. Offers came. And then, so did the money.

Ending her eighteen-year marriage was the ceremonious shedding of an outgrown skin. She'd never relied on David for her happiness, but never dreamed he would try to make her unhappy, until it happened. With every passing day, he pulled further and further away from her, and nothing she tried could bring him back. How many times, in how many ways, had she opened herself up to him, reached out to him? How many times was she given excuse after excuse for his emotional distance, and then, his cruelty? The number was high, and she'd made the decision early on to leave it uncounted.

He came to her only when he wanted something. Then, he took. Then, he turned away.

It hadn't been that way in the beginning. When they first met, he was sweet and attentive, kind and giving. Her dreams were his dreams. They both wanted the same things. They were perfect for each other, in the beginning. But the man she'd fallen in love with disappeared; slowly, steadily, completely. It took years of heartache and a lot of soul searching before she could bring herself to face the fact that he hadn't even changed. He'd merely stopped hiding who he really was.

She'd stayed for one reason, because of the only good thing he had given her: a family. She'd stayed for their son, Shawn; swallowing her emotions, her passions, her pride, so that he could grow up in a stable, two-parent home. But even the day-to-day bliss of raising a child was diluted by her cascading feelings for David. Love turned to disappointment. Disappointment turned to grief. Grief turned to apathy. The only reason he'd stayed was because he was afraid of being alone.

There was a saying she'd read once and barely remembered, about trusting the timing in life. When Shawn left their house for college, it felt empty, sad, lifeless, like her marriage. She took it as a sign. When Shaylee told David she was leaving, he looked at her with contempt. He sneered hateful words. He told her what she could and couldn't take out of the house, but didn't ask why she was leaving. For that, she was grateful. She wasn't sure how to explain to him that he'd made their relationship feel like a series of one-night stands.

Two years later, Shaylee released her first novel. The critics praised it. Her existing fans loved it. The novel earned her more than a million new fans and secured her writing career. She bought a beautiful piece of hilltop property. It was secluded, but still only a twenty-minute drive from her hometown, Battleground. Near a stand of wild cherry trees was the perfect spot for her guest cottage. She lived in it while she watched the home she'd envisioned all her life take shape.

It had a big, beautiful, sun-lit kitchen. There were skylights everywhere. The dining room was ample but cozy. French doors opened out from the dining area to an enclosed porch. It faced north, and so stayed cool during the summer. The living room was filled with comfortable, overstuffed furniture. Sliding glass doors led from the living room to an open deck on the house's southeast side. It was a peaceful vantage point to watch the sunrises. The deck also captured any heat the sun was willing to give up on short winter days. Between the two rooms sat a large, raised, open fireplace with a built-in barbecue.

An atrium separated two junior suites from her office. The first floor also held an inviting master guest suite with a private entrance. It had two fireplaces. One separated a sleeping area from a sitting area. The other was in a luxury spa-style bathroom.

Wide stairs led down to her own master suite, a mirror image of the first-floor guest suite. It was on the lower level and at the back of the house. With a separate entrance and kitchen, it allowed for privacy; hers, and her guests.

As the house was being constructed, anticipation was also raised; built into the walls, mixed in with the paint. She would host countless events for her family and friends. Her home would be filled with interesting new people. Her days would be filled with fascinating adventures. And her nights? They would hold intrigue and romance. Catered affairs, elaborate parties, and travel excursions would fill her social calendar for years to come.

But nothing like that happened. What did happen, what time proved, was that nothing would change, that everything would go on as it had before. The people already in her life made room for her a few times a year, inside special gatherings or on major holidays. Those celebrations were wonderful, but always too short, with too much time between them. She'd all but given up on making friends. None of her attempts to welcome new people into her circle went well. She was met with poorly concealed bitterness, shadowed animosity, and just-below-the-surface envy.

And all those just around the corner romances she'd imagined; the ones she dreamed of, even written about? Where were those clever, charming men with arms full of roses and eyes full of adventure? Nowhere near her front door. The ones who did approach her were conniving, grasping, and desperate. They had the singular attitude that their blunt tools of transparent charm and practiced lies would open her arms, her heart, and her bank book.

Why were so many so quick to judge, to covet?

She'd worked a lifetime to perfect her writing skills. She'd also battled demons, overcome obstacles, and fought nameless, faceless fears. Nothing she'd ever wanted had been handed to her. It had been pulled, kicking and screaming, out of the arms of a harsh and critical world. For her, paying dues wasn't just a concept. For her, it had always been a way of life. There were a few who understood. The rest refused to.

Being a strong woman, she thought she would attract other strong people, but the opposite was true. Those who came to her were fragile, afraid, and looking for protection. She tried to love them. She tried to be a positive presence, to build them up. But their fears, their weaknesses and insecurities were stronger than her love. They couldn't stop themselves from trying to tear her down.

She couldn't blame anyone but herself for mistakes she'd made over and over again. She wouldn't blame anyone else for letting those mistakes hurt her. But, after giving too many people too many chances, after being left sore and aching too many times, she started making new plans, for one. And Shawn: her son, her only child, her truest love? For every one of her invitations, he had equal and opposite excuses to decline them. She took her first trip overseas, to Italy, alone.

Determined to concentrate on what she did have, Shaylee looked for the little miracles of everyday life. Some of them, she found: a green field dotted yellow with blooming dandelions, a place along the river where she watched a hawk bathe in the river and dry its feathers in the wind. Others found their way to her: wild sunflowers that grew where she'd spilled some birdseed, warm summer rains, branches that reached out to touch her on walks through the forest.

She focused on her privacy, not her isolation. She counted her blessings, not her failures, her biggest blessing being her work. It was her work that filled her with passion, even if it was only imaginings finding their way from her mind onto paper or into her computer. It was her work that filled her with purpose, even if it was to make other people happy while she struggled through too many types of sadness. And, her work had handed her a new blessing, a new adventure. James Vincent was coming to see her. On Monday, James Vincent was coming to see her.

# The First Chapter

A stoic hotel manager escorted Shaylee to the penthouse. He stood silent watch beside her until the door opened. James Vincent was, in person, more handsome than on any screen. The skin of his face wasn't as flawless as it looked on his show or in his movies (probably make-up and lighting). But its slight imperfections only made her want to reach out and smooth them away with her fingers. His eyes were steel-blue. A spirited intelligence radiated from behind them. A perfect amount of creases framed them. Silver streaks reflected in and out of his dark hair as he moved, highlights that seemed painted in.

The smile he gave her was thin and formal. His grip on the doorknob was white-knuckled. It looked painful. He stepped back away from the doorway to let her in but didn't loosen his grip on the knob. Once she was inside, he nodded to the manager and shut the door. James Vincent let go of the doorknob, stretched the hand open, shook it, and stretched it out again. Apparently, it had been as painful as it looked.

His face paled and his eyes widened as he offered in a tight, strained voice, "Have a seat."

He bent forward slightly, sweeping open his left arm. Meant to be an inviting gesture to guide her further into the room, the movement was stiff and mechanical; his own anxiety catching in his joints.

'Why is he so nervous?' she wondered.

Shaylee sat down at an antique mahogany table. He took the seat across from her. Their eyes met, and, in that moment, she felt her every imperfection. She remembered she'd just turned forty-four. That she'd started to dye her hair because the grays had formed a plot to overtake her head. That every morning her mirror reminded her of the lines on her face getting a little deeper, the skin over her eyes drooping a little lower. She was a little overweight. Her lips were too thin. He was only six years younger, but . . .

'Stop it, Shaylee. Just stop it,' she caught hold of her runaway thoughts. 'He asked you here because you are a good writer, a really good writer. A professional, successful writer. Remember that. Re-mem-ber that.'

The rustling sounds of pulling a new notebook out of her purse were a conspicuous noise in the quiet room. Even the act of setting it down on the table was audible. A frustrated sigh escaped through an embarrassed smile while she dug around the bottom of that vacuous purse in search of a pen. When, finally, the pen was captured and placed triumphantly on top of the notebook, she offered an explanation.

"I'll be using a digital recorder for most of our interviews, but, for now, I want to use hand-written notes. Writing notes out on paper will help me form a better mental picture of the outline."

He sat ramrod straight, elbows pointed out, hands clenching the chair's arms. A slight nod of acknowledgment was his only movement.

"So, James," she tried to begin.

"Jim," he interrupted. "Please. Jim. I'm Jim."

Shaylee corrected herself. "So, Jim, why does it feel like you're more nervous than I am?"

"Well, yes. I am. A little. Nervous." His next breath, deep and controlled, was released with the words, "Shaylee is a very pretty name."

"Thank you." She felt herself blush at the unexpected compliment. "It was a combination of married names on my mother's side. My great-grandmother married into the 'Shay' family. My grandmother married a man whose last name was 'Lee.'"

His gaze moved from her eyes to her flushed cheeks. Her explanation finished, he looked down and spoke to the top of the table.

"Yes. Good. Good. Please, Shaylee, please, please, keep talking. Yes. This is great. This is what I want. When I agreed to do this, I didn't realize how hard it might be to share the private details of my life with someone."

He looked up and focused his full attention on her. "Then, I saw you at the door, and, it all became real. I think it's going to take me some time to get comfortable with this. After all," his eyebrows rose with exaggerated suggestiveness, "I'll be sharing some of my deepest, darkest secrets with you."

She responded with a nervous laugh. The attempted humor was strained, but it lightened the mood. Her first official question easily slid out.

"I'm curious. Do you have any ideas for your book's title?"

"I'm not sure. I've thought about it a little, but I'm just not sure. I love being an actor. I love the excitement, and the action, but the day-to-day part of the job, it's never easy. Long, erratic hours. Deadlines making everyone crazy. Scenes and lines to memorize. Scenes and lines to forget once they're recorded. Multiple bosses to deal with. Crews coming and going. Sets coming and going. All that uncertainty. No two days are ever the same."

He fidgeted in the confines of his chair, but the words easily escaped.

"Nothing is permanent, Shaylee. Nothing. I'll go years at a time without work and then have to shift into mad focus overnight when I do land a role. The work is real. The results are real, but the process doesn't feel that way. Maybe, because I'm only one small part of it. Even if I'm the star of the show, I'm still only one person in a cast. I might be getting a bigger salary or a bigger dressing room, but the salary stops. The dressing room goes away. The people I work with disappear. It all disappears.

"I guess what I think is missing is something concrete, something lasting. Something I can hold onto, and keep."

As he opened up to her, Shaylee's intentions teased around the edges of her mind, until they touched on the need to reassure him.

"This book," she promised, "will not be a done-to-death analogy. It won't be a collection of time-worn clichés, either. What it will be is a poignant, honest account of the personal life and career path of a successful man.

"To do that, I need to let myself see you as a person, as the man you are, not the legend you've become. And I, I need you," she paused to look into his eyes, "to see me as an ally, maybe even a friend, not a curious stranger with a notebook and a mission."

With a smile, she tried to soften her next words, hoping they would sound more like a request than a demand.

"I want to learn everything about you, and I want to learn it from you. I haven't done any outside research, and I don't want to. All you have to do is share it with me, Jim, share your life with me. Share everything with me, and I can promise you it will be real. This story will be real, something you can hold onto."

She waited, to gauge his reaction. The concern left his eyes, and they softened. His slight nod confirmed he believed, or wanted to believe, what she was saying.

A timid knock on the door brought James Vi . . ., Jim, to his feet. He opened it to a tall, postured man proudly wearing his bright white uniform. The red name tag on his spotless jacket identified him as Rolf Vonderohe, Executive Chef.

Rolf guided the cart in front of him to the center of the room. Shaylee stood up to get a better look, and Jim repositioned their chairs around it. Centered on the cart was a beautifully prepared tray of appetizers. Piled up around the tray were fresh, dewy flowers mingled with unblemished whole fruits. Foil-wrapped hard candies added sparkling accents to the impressive display.

From underneath the cart appeared a small side table. It was added to the cozy seating arrangement. A silver-plated ice bucket also appeared and was set onto the little table. The final detail was two sparkling clean glasses. They rang with the subtle echo of fine crystal as they were moved into place. With a signature, the man was gone.

Jim pulled one of the chairs out for her. The surprised look on her face pleased him. Her enjoyment of the luxurious treats pleased him. His attention, his smile, his engaging small talk, they were all things that pleased her.

The longer they talked, the more relaxed Jim became. As he relaxed, his voice became richer, deeper. It was the voice she recognized, the one he was known for.

With the food picked over and the bottle half empty, they moved their chairs back to the antique table. Shaylee picked up her pen and notebook. Jim began with a simple biography. He spoke haltingly, trying to give her enough time to write everything down.

"Full name, James Michael Vincent. Single. Never married. No kids. Not in a relationship. Raised in Philadelphia, Pennsylvania. Germantown area. From a big, traditional Roman Catholic family. Six brothers, two sisters. I'm the youngest, the seventh son. My dad was also a seventh son.

"Less than a year after I was born, Mom turned thirty-five, and announced she'd gone into "early menopause." That's Catholic speak for, 'I'm on birth control now,' so I was the last and youngest child. Seventh son and done. But still, nine kids is a respectable size for a Roman Catholic family, right?"

He laughed, and it sounded as though velvet had been given a voice.

¤ ¤ ¤ ¤ ¤ ¤ ¤ ¤ ¤ ¤ ¤ ¤ ¤ ¤

Monday was their introduction. Tuesday was Portland. Shaylee walked him around the area near his hotel, The Pearl District. Jim was entranced. The revitalized commercial district's architecture ran the gamut. Renovated factories and remodeled industrial complexes filled entire city blocks. New brick townhomes were surrounded by art galleries, boutiques, and unique eateries. High-rise buildings punctuated the scenery like exclamation points.

On Wednesday, Shaylee pulled up in front of the hotel. Jim took in the sight of her shimmering lavender all-terrain vehicle, a quizzical look on his face. He noticed the custom tapestry upholstery before sitting down, but said nothing. He stared down at the purple glitter floor mats under his feet without commenting.

They traveled up the Columbia River Gorge. Jim shook his head in stunned silence as every bend in the road showed him a scene more beautiful than the last.

At the first look-out point, he said, "I think this is the most beautiful view of Mount Hood I've ever seen." But they passed Beacon Rock and he corrected himself. "No. I was wrong. This is the most beautiful view of Mount Hood I've ever seen."

"Wrong again," he laughed on their drive back towards the city lights at sunset. The gorge filled with a rich golden light that saturated everything it touched. And then, the sky took over. It flared brilliant scarlet and aged to a mellow orange that silhouetted the skyline. The sun disappeared. The river, the hills, and the mountain faded into layered purple shadows behind them.

On Thursday morning, Shaylee filled two coolers. One with food, the other with bottled water and juices. While collecting up snacks, she took some time to enjoy the anticipation of the day ahead. Jim only knew that they were going on another drive, but not where.

He searched the passing landscapes for clues. She was rewarded with a beaming smile when a wayside sign answered the question.

The road leading to Mount Saint Helens was an experience all its own. High cliffs, deep ravines. Blue shadowed hills in the distance, lush green forests surrounding them. At any moment you could go from admiring the scenery to becoming a part of it.

Past Lake Merwin and Yale Lake, through the little town of Cougar. The official viewpoint sites, Harmony, Smith Creek, Windy Ridge, were crowded with tourists. Shaylee passed by them and found the entrance to an abandoned logging area.

Ahead of them rose an access road carved into a hillside. The surface of the single lane pathway was rough with crushed shale rock. It wrapped around the hill like a languid snake.

As she changed gears, a fearful look crossed Jim's face. There was lighthearted reassurance in her words. "Well, this is why I have a four-wheel-drive S.U.V."

"Why is it purple?" he jumped on the first opportunity to question her color choice.

"You never know when you might need to blend in with a herd of elephants."

Jim was on the verge of a chuckle, but it was tossed out of his throat by a gasp as they lurched forward to meet the hill. He grabbed the roof handle (what everyone she knew growing up called the "Oh, shit!" grip.) and held tight. Wide tires dug into the gravel, making loud crunching and popping noises. The engine revved as the heavy vehicle strained to rise. Dried puddles and ruts made for a slow and jarring ride. They rounded the back of the hill to find a mudslide blocking their way.

"This is as far as we can go," she announced, not at all disappointed by the view.

St. Helens sat in a deep valley, up to her hips in thick white fog. Only the tops of the tallest trees were visible proof she was attached to the earth. Gold light from the late morning sun added a wistful quality. The vista hinted at possibility, that the mountain might rise into the sky and fly away at any moment. It could have been the scene from a fairytale, but it wasn't. It was for anyone lucky enough to have ventured into God's Country.

Shaylee hopped out to survey the area. Jim sat, unmoving, pale, showing her another white-knuckled grip. She turned away to enjoy a private smile. City boys.

An appreciative smile came to her face when she opened up the back of her purple sports utility vehicle. Lush upholstery fabric gave the roomy compartment a romantic, medieval look. The detailed flower pattern was dominated by shades of rich mauve and dusty lavender. Accent colors included aged rose and shadowy cream.

"Come on, Jim. We can sit here." She slapped the lowered gate before climbing inside.

He stood by as she retrieve the pillows, snacks, and ice-cold drinks that would create a cozy nest.

"But really," his question fell in with the sounds of her arranging and rearranging, "why purple?"

"I guess you didn't do any research on me, did you, Jim?"

His blurted "What?" was followed by a guilty nod that dropped his gaze to his shoes. "Well, um. . ."

Shaylee sensed a weak apology coming on, and spoke over his uncomfortable silence.

"Purple is my favorite color, and tapestry," she sat down and opened her laptop, "it's my favorite fabric."

An understanding look came to his face. "Oh, I get it now."

Jim's stories paired well with the volcano view in that quiet, out-of-the-way place. She listened to his voice all afternoon. It filled the air with sound and her mind with ideas.

On the trip back down the gravel road, there was one minor skidding incident. It rattled even an experienced driver like Shaylee. For a few panicked seconds, she imagined them careening off the path and plunging to their deaths. But it was just one slip, just one moment. The tires caught, the vehicle steadied, and the feeling was forgotten when they leveled out at the bottom of the hill.

Leaving the forest was always sadly sweet for Shaylee. The long drive gave her time to relive the day, and, mourn its ending. Jim was quiet, looking out the window. He had no idea of the contrast of feelings she was experiencing. The road had guided her to one of the most ruggedly beautiful places in her world. It now ushered her away, towards the familiar safety of home.

Stomach rumblings interrupted her indulgent thoughts. They reminded her dinner was waiting in the cooler. Just ahead was a familiar landmark. She pulled over, to an area that had been cleared of trees. While looking for a spot to lay out a picnic blanket, she walked into a stand of wild black raspberries.

Juicy berries warmed by the sun made a sweet side dish. They added to the flavor of the day, and to a meal of spiral cut ham with homemade potato salad.

"These, what did you call them?" Jim asked.

"Blackcaps," she explained between bites.

"These blackcaps are great, Shaylee."

The clear-cut around them was dotted with tree stumps and littered with abandoned logs. Undisturbed forest surrounded the thirty or so acre area. It was a spot she knew well, one of the places she'd spent her childhood exploring. Back then, branch piles were mountains meant to be climbed. Craters left by logging equipment were undiscovered valleys in need of exploring. Their adventures were accompanied by the perfumes of mossy earth and fresh-cut wood. Now it was sun-bleached, vine-covered, and dusty.

Across the road and down a steep incline was Swift Reservoir. She knew that she would soon see an Osprey flying over the glassy surface of the water, hunting for fish. She knew the berries they were eating would usually have been gone. But, because of a late, cold spring, the summer's heat was kept at bay, and the season had been extended. She also knew that if she looked around, she'd find another kind of berry for Jim to sample.

While he filled an empty water bottle with black caps, Shaylee hunted for dewberries. The low-growing vines were hard to find, and the berries were small, but the tart and tasty fruit was worth the effort.

Their stomachs, and the cooler, stuffed with found fruit, they continued the drive back to civilization. Along the way, they made plans for a day trip to Newport, Oregon.

Friday was a blur of ocean views, vanity shops, and seafood restaurants. Stories bounced back and forth between them with the speed of excited pinballs when they talked about one of the things they had in common: Philadelphia, Pennsylvania. Shaylee had spent five years there. Four in the Navy, working at the Philadelphia Naval Base, and another year as a live-in tourist.

She'd lost hours, sometimes whole days, wandering the city's oldest, most historic streets. The cobblestone mazes were lined with parks, statues, fountains, museums, and libraries. Diverse architecture spanned three centuries. On one block were tiny colonial brick homes built in the seventeen-hundreds. At the next corner stood a chiseled stone chapel constructed in Eighteen-Eighty. Only a few streets away were modern giants with bones of steel and skins of glass.

The sun went down, and lamp light exposed another side of life. Restaurant, bar, and theater patrons spilled onto and off of the main sidewalks. They were entertained by street musicians and tempted by vendors. Folding tables and rolling carts held makeshift displays. Clothing, jewelry, knock-off handbags, electronics, pirated music and movies, sunglasses, toys. Cash only and don't ask where they came from.

Narrow side streets that light couldn't reach belonged to drug dealers, prostitutes, and thieves. They were havens for the homeless, destinations for the lost. What the city tried to hide at night was just as fascinating as what it revealed during the day. All of it, different from anything Shaylee had ever known.

She mentioned something she'd never liked about Philly and Jim was quick to agree. The fact that there was nowhere to be alone. Every road, sidewalk, side street, every alley, park bench, and corner. They were within view of or occupied by someone, always. Even at night. Walking along what looked like lonely streets, there were voices in the distance, faces in the shadows.

One story led to another. One hour led to another. A late dinner of clam chowder and bakery rolls was quickly eaten, barely tasted. Empty bowls were replaced with frosty mugs of apricot ale. So intent was their conversation that they didn't notice the day ending around them.

The restaurant emptied and quieted. The sun went down. Ocean sounds met them at the door and a dark sky full of misted stars escorted them out of town. Highway 101 North led away from Newport, towards Lincoln City. The casino lights were clearly visible from the road, and too tempting to just pass by.

Together, they walked in through the casino doors. Jim was immediately recognized by an elderly woman walking out.

"Oh, my. James Vincent. You're James Vincent."

Her shrill call of recognition caught the attention of a floor boss and a waitress. Jim warmly greeted the woman, who identified herself as Violet Davis. Shaylee smiled, trying to show interest in their conversation, but inside the casino, heads were turning. A group of employees was forming.

A tall, slender man in a tailored suit approached the growing crowd. She wasn't close enough to hear but could see that the employees all talked to him at once. What a confusion of excited explanations the man must have been confronted with. He deciphered something intelligible from the mayhem and turned towards them. His eyes squarely on Jim, he adjusted his sleeve cuffs and straightened his tie as he approached.

Violet was on the move again, holding an enthusiastic conversation with herself. She alternated her attention between the autograph in her hand and the doors opening ahead of her. "James Vincent. I can't believe it. I can't believe I just met James Vincent. Oh, just wait until the girls at . . ." The chatter was cut off when the doors closed behind her.

"Mr. Vincent?" the man in the suit asked. "Mr. James Vincent?"

Jim responded with a smooth and practiced, "Yes."

"Of course. Welcome, Mr. Vincent. Welcome. I'm Len. Your host."

As Jim shook his extended hand, Len asked in a controlled and professional voice, "How may I help you this evening?"

Jim scanned the bright, noisy room. "Where are the Roulette Wheels?"

The pitch of Len's voice rose slightly. "Yes. Yes. Please, follow me." As an afterthought, he added, in a lower voice, "and Madam," without bothering to look at her. Jim followed Len towards the back of the room. She followed Jim. Two waitresses rushed up to them, then slowed their pace to follow behind her.

Their entourage snaked through a maze of video poker machines and craps tables. When they reached the Roulette wheels, Len stepped away. The waitresses passed Shaylee and fanned out. They positioned themselves, one on either side of Jim, and escorted him to the edge of the table. He looked over the wheel and its table before turning to Shaylee, a perfect smile on his face.

"Shaylee, how are you at being a good luck charm?" The tone of his voice was playful. His head tilted playfully when his steel-blue eyes motioned to the spot next to him.

She almost looked around to see who he was talking to, but caught herself. Nine careful, decisive steps brought her to the spot he'd chosen. The young, dyed-blonde waitress to his left stepped back. The girl confirmed, with a quick glance, that Jim wasn't looking. Her pasted-on smile transformed into a nasty glare meant only for Shaylee. The urge to respond with a smirk was strong, but she resisted. Impressed by her own self-control, she took a deep breath. Her focus slipped away from the displaced waitress, and to the man beside her.

Most of the employees were kind enough to include her in their fawning, but their attentions were centered on Jim. To her, all the fuss was flustering and uncomfortable. But Jim bought chips, made bets, and ordered drinks, relaxed, unruffled, unaffected. Just a normal night out.

Shaylee didn't play the wheel. It was hard enough to figure out the confusion around her. There were low moans of disappointment when Jim lost and cheers when he won. Trays filled with drinks and appetizers appeared out of nowhere. People materialized from, and then disappeared into, a background sea of faces, but not Len. He'd posted himself an arms-length from Jim and didn't relinquish that spot the entire night. His looks, nods, and gestures smoothly orchestrated everything happening around them. Several times, when he thought no one was looking, he discretely and eagerly eyed the growing stacks of chips.

She gave Jim a sidelong glance. It had been four days since they'd met; four twelve-hour days. All the time they'd spent together, all the stories they'd shared, and she couldn't find her way past his image, or, through her awe of him. He was fighting his own battle of self-consciousness but was well aware of hers. When they were alone, his movements were controlled and subtle. He spoke quietly, deliberately, carefully, as though she was a shy bird he was trying not to startle.

He was different from the Jim at the Roulette wheel. This Jim was comfortable in unfamiliar surroundings. He interacted easily with everyone around him. He was lively and animated. This Jim was the man she needed to get to know. To do her best work, it was the version of him she needed to understand.

The evening passed by as all their time together had, in a slow-motion, dreamlike blur. The trance was gently broken with Jim's breezy announcement. "Well, it's almost midnight. Time to wrap this up. I think I've taken enough of the casino's money."

Echoes of laughter skipped through the crowd. For some reason, Shaylee expected applause, but there was none. Only the mumble of voices and the shuffling of feet as onlookers dispersed.

Several chips went to the dealer. Jim searched the crowd in an attempt to find the waitresses but didn't have to look far. She tried not to notice how much he gave them, but the expressions on their faces showed him to be generous.

He gathered his remaining chips before approaching Len. They exchanged a few hushed words, and Jim gave him his tip. Jim's hands were noticeably emptier, and Len's smile was noticeably bigger.

The cage was within view, but every few steps, a fan approached to congratulate him on his winnings. He engaged in small talk, answered questions, and easily charmed everyone he spoke with. Another half-hour passed before Jim was able to cash in his remaining chips.

With a three-hour drive ahead of them, there wouldn't be time for even a quick go at one of the video poker machines. She imagined how that might have gone. Her losing almost every hand and a bored Jim watching her lose almost every hand. It was a good thing they were running late.

Because she hadn't gotten to bed until after four a.m., Friday started with a late lunch at a bistro near Jim's hotel. Over a meal of delicately flavored clam cakes and minted fruit salad, Shaylee gave him a flash drive. On it was a copy of the interviews she'd managed to type up, along with some of her notes and ideas. Once they were in Jim's suite, he copied everything onto his computer. They went over the information together, spending the rest of the day on their laptops. And so began James Vincent's as-told-to autobiography, "Holding Tinsel In My Hands."

Saturday was left to chance. From the hotel, they started out on foot. There was no need to discuss lunch plans. They only had to follow their sense of smell to the nearest bakery, a thickly painted black and white cinder block building. In a past life, it might have been a gas station or an auto repair shop.

Once they were inside, chunky, oversized windows framed a fountain in a concrete park. Crowded around it was a large group of people. As their waitress approached, Shaylee smiled. Portland never disappointed. The painfully thin woman sported spiked orange hair, gaudy tattoos, and multiple piercings.

Shaylee asked, "Do you know what's going on at the fountain?"

She was rewarded with a contemptuous glare and a growled, "Don't ask me."

The scowl on that pinched face would have deepened even more if she'd known the comment had cost her a big tip.

Shaylee tried to enjoy her meal. The roast beef sandwich was tasty. The snow pea and fennel bulb slaw was sweet and crunchy. But her impatience fueled a subtle feeding frenzy. Jim's jaws moved at a fast pace too. They looked out the window as they ate.

In even the short time it took them to finish, the gathering had grown. It took a lot of maneuvering and many excuse me's to pick their way through the randomly spaced groups of people. Jim came into view of the fountain first and let out a one-word exclamation. "Wow."

Shaylee was a few steps behind, and almost a foot below him. She had to move around one more person to share his view. Boats. Toy boats. The fountain was alive with them. She felt herself begin to smile. Jim was smiling too, a look of confused pleasure on his face as he confessed, "I've never seen anything like this."

Out loud, she wondered, "Is this is some kind of competition?"

A female voice within earshot offered in a Jamaican accent, "Oh, no, nothing like that. On hot days, some of the parents bring their kids out here to play in the fountain. Today it looks like everybody brought their toys. Isn't it adorable?"

Some of the boats were attached to their owners by strings. Others were free-floating. Some were plastic. Others were wood. Painted or plain, simple or intricate, store-bought or handmade, they all delightfully filled the fountain. Sporadic waves aimlessly pushed them together, pulled them apart, or sent them spinning. When the sun was behind the clouds, the water was bluish-gray. When the sun was allowed to shine, all the little boats sailed on a sea of glitter.

Roses blooming throughout the park offered their perfume to the air; moist, warm air too heavy for a breeze. Splattering sounds from the falling water blended with the hum of voices. Shaylee was able to pick out fragments of conversations.

Two young girls in front of her were choosing their favorites. "Oh, look at that big red one." "I like that blue one. The one with the little white flag." "Oh, I see it. That one's cute, too."

A pair of boys, who looked to be brothers close in age, were kneeling together over the water, arguing. "Aw, Chad, you sunk my boat." "No way. No way. It's not my fault. Here, try again." They reached into the water and grabbed the boat at the same time, spawning another round of blame and denial.

A father's instructions: "Let up on the string, Jeremy! There you go son, you did it. You caught a wave."

An entranced man: "Look at that one. It must have taken hours, days, maybe even weeks, to put that one together. What do you think, Donna?" A patient wife's answer: "Yes, Clyde. I think you're right. Probably weeks."

A group of five teenagers walked past, bored looks pasted on their faces. One of them hung back to sneak a few curious glances. She caught up to her friends and let her face go expressionless again.

"Jim, what do you think?"

"Amazing," he answered without taking his eyes off the fountain. "Just, amazing."

Shaylee stopped people-watching to join Jim in his appreciation of the miniature flotilla. It was something she couldn't remember seeing before, and might not see again.

For a while, they held their ground, but Shaylee felt people brushing past her. The gaps around them were filling in. Standing in the same spot, they were losing sight of the fountain.

"Time to go?" she asked.

Disappointment crossed his face. A slight pout came and went almost before she noticed it. Because she knew Jim wouldn't be able to hear it over the noise, she allowed herself a quiet chuckle. The only difference between men and boys: shoe size.

He sighed out, "Time to go," and scanned the sea of heads to find an escape route. "This way. Follow me," he directed, picking a way for them through the gathering. They wove a crooked path to an empty sidewalk and followed it out of the park. The sounds of splashing water and enthusiastic voices faded behind them. Beautiful noises were replaced with less enchanting city din. A slight tug in her chest told her how she'd been affected. She'd just made a memory she would visit many times.

Before leaving the hotel, Jim asked Shaylee to leave her notebook and recorder behind. It was awkward at first, empty hands and a full mind. But, with nothing but the day between them, she found her first real opportunity to focus on Jim, the person.

There was nothing subtle about his presence, but even though it was strong, it wasn't formidable. The way he held himself, the way he moved and spoke. His whole attitude was one of confidence, but there was nothing arrogant about him. He wasn't childish or immature, but there was an innocence to him, a quality that added to his unique charm. How had he managed to keep life, and Hollywood, from stealing that innocence away?

Their week together was meant for her to learn about him. It was also meant to replace pre-conceived ideas with first-hand observations. There was a lot he would keep hidden, but she was curious to see how much he would reveal. Shaylee was noticing those bits and pieces of himself he'd added to his movie characters. She was learning that he was nothing like his reality show persona. She was coming to understand the roles he'd played were not who he was. They might have been well-written and skillfully acted. They might have given birth to Jim, the legend, but were in no way like Jim, the man.

She got an insight into Jim, the man, when they came across a homeless teenager. The boy had neatly cut hair, but his face was unshaven and dirty. His clothes were new, but stained with the proof of many nights on the streets. He was young, but wore a hardened expression; his dark eyes at the same time cold and angry. The moment those eyes focused on her, Jim tensed. She saw, in profile, that his full attention was on the stranger: shoulders squared, back straight, jaw set, lips pressed tightly into a thin line.

"It's okay," she said quietly out of the corner of her mouth, but the words did nothing to dissuade him. With gentle nudges, their arms barely touching, Jim guided her even further around him. Only after a distance of five blocks and three perimeter checks did he seem to relax a little. But his deliberate stance made it clear he was aware of everything going on around them. It also left no room for doubt that she was well protected.

It was not a day to hurry. It was a day meant to pass at its own pace. Sometimes, they laughed together. Other times, they took turns. Sometimes they both tried to talk at once. Other times, they walked in silence. They didn't pay attention to where they'd come from or where they were going. Shaylee just took in the mood, the city, and Jim's company.

The sun disappeared behind Portland's west hills. Shaylee was again amazed by how easy it was to lose track of time when she and Jim were together. She didn't want the walk to end but her feet had their own opinion. Without confessing her pain, she told Jim, "I hate to admit it, but I'm starting to get tired."

He pulled a business card out of his shirt pocket: Radio Cab Company. "Shaylee, I left my phone at the hotel. You've got yours with you, right?"

They found a bench, made the call, and decided on Chinese food for dinner while they waited for a taxi. Their driver, George, was blonde, thick-boned, and heavy-set. Bright blue eyes and pale lashes gave his face a surprised look, but a warm smile softened his startled gaze. He recognized Jim, but tried to hide his obvious delight with a casually tossed, "Where ya headed?"

"This is my favorite place," George offered as they pulled up to a Chinatown restaurant. "And," he laughed, patting his ample abdomen, "as you can see, I've had more than my share of good Chinese food."

Shaylee laughed politely before she got out of the cab. Jim asked her to go in and find them a table, staying behind with George. It was several minutes before he joined her in the booth she'd picked.

"I know you're tired, so I asked him to wait for us," was his simple explanation.

Two half-finished pu pu platters and one empty teapot later, Jim brought up the subject of the book.

"I love your ideas, Shaylee. All of them. I can't wait to get started. Last night I made some schedule changes. Is next Sunday too soon, to start?"

She laughed. "Too soon? No. It doesn't seem soon enough. I've got a million ideas going through my head. But, now that I think about it, I still have all our recorded interviews to transcribe. That might take a week."

"I wanted you to have enough time to do that, so, good. That's perfect. Next Sunday. Next Sunday it is."

The check and two fortune cookies arrived on a chipped and scratched black plastic tray. Shaylee picked up one of the cookies. Jim picked up the remaining cookie and the check.

He opened the plastic wrapper, and tried to gently pry the cookie apart, but it crumbled out of his hands, onto his plate. While fishing the fortune out of the leftovers, he offered, "I'll book a room at the Vancouver Hilton. Maybe I should reserve a conference room for us to work in."

As he read to himself, Shaylee insisted, "No, Jim, we don't need a hotel conference room. You're more than welcome to work at my place. I have a great office."

He looked up. "Wow. Really? Thank you. That would be great. More private, and, I'll bet, prettier."

His smile faltered. He seemed a little embarrassed by what he'd just said. "Than a conference room, I mean. Your office is prettier than a conference room."

"Yes," Shaylee agreed absentmindedly, "it probably is."

She was focused on her favorite part of any Chinese meal: the reading of the fortune. The cookie opened with a snap. Out loud, she read, "The journey of a thousand miles begins with one step."

Jim continued. "Then I guess I'll rent a car and drive back and forth."

"Perfect," she answered, gazing curiously at the soggy little strip of paper Jim held. "Well, what does yours say?"

"Mine. Well, um, mine says, 'The time will come for you to reveal a secret.'"

"Really?"

Jim nodded.

"Oh my," intrigue deepened her voice, "then I guess it's official. A journey will be taken, and," she paused for a teasing smile and continued in a stage whisper, "a secret will be shared."

Jim didn't answer. He didn't smile. He just nodded, again.

Shaylee looked out of the restaurant's glass door. The street lights were on but glowed dim in a hazy twilight. Almost directly across the street was their cab.

Jim ushered her to it and opened the door for her, his eyes searching the area around them. He closed it firmly before walking around the back of the car to get in on the other side.

As Jim sat down beside her, George quickly rubbed a wad of napkins over his mouth and chin. Beside him were three open take-out containers. After a hasty swallow, he managed, "Thanks for the grub, Mr. Vincent."

Jim nodded as he closed his own door. Shaylee sat looking straight ahead but was thinking of the man beside her. Not only had he shown concern for her, he'd taken the time, and the effort, to make sure their cabbie was taken care of too.

On Sunday morning, Shaylee pulled up in front of the hotel. She expected to wait for Jim, but he rushed out of the building with an uncomfortable look on his face. Following him was a petite and slender young man in a porter's uniform. He was trying to catch up, but was slowed by the weight of Jim's suitcases. They reached her car and the employee's sparkling eyes and seductive smile explained all.

Every part of him faced Jim, even as he tossed the luggage into the back seat and shut the door. Freed of his burden, he glided towards his object of desire, who raised a crisp hundred dollar bill between them. The enamored doorman was stunned into motionless silence. Jim pressed the bill into his hand and slipped around him.

Shaylee's greeting was a knowing smile. Jim's was a relieved sigh, almost lost in the frantic noises of closing and locking his own door. She pulled away, leaving the crestfallen man looking after them from the curb.

Rehashing his harrowing escape had them both giddy, but Jim interrupted their third round of laughter. "Seriously though, we need to go over our plans. I won't have any time to talk to you once my plane is in the air."

"Ah, yes. You're right," she agreed, staying on-topic until they reached the security gate.

"Okay, Shaylee, thanks for everything. I'll see you next week."

"Yes, next week, and Jim?"

"What?"

"Beware of bellhops bearing gifts."

They were laughing when she turned to start the long walk to the short-term parking lot. About halfway back through the terminal hallway, she was startled by a loud noise behind her. Without thinking, she turned around. She didn't see what caused the sound, but did see Jim. He was standing to one side of the security line, watching her. He smiled an innocent smile and waved. She returned his smile and waved back.

A question crossed her mind. She felt it cross her face. A group of people swarmed around from behind her, moving towards the gate, and she lost sight of him. Her arm dropped down to her side and the question was forgotten. It was chased out of her mind by the immediate panic of all the work and errands that needed to be done in less than a week. On the way to the car, she started a mental to-do list. The longer the list got, the quicker she walked.

¤ ¤ ¤ ¤ ¤ ¤ ¤ ¤ ¤ ¤ ¤ ¤ ¤ ¤

Shaylee approached the tidy little post-war house converted into an office. A neatly centered sign in the small yard read, "Joseph McConaughey, Attorney at Law."

Joseph (Never call him Joe.) was as Irish as any man could be. A thick accent. Bright red hair. Short of stature. Squinting eyes. Freckles spilling off a pale face. He sported an eternal smile that leaked his obvious lust for life.

Shaylee loved her visits with Joseph. His enthusiasm was inspiring, and on this day, she needed a lake of that enthusiasm to swim in. She'd worked as a legal secretary for six years, but those attorneys were her employers. Their cases were other people's. Facing her own legalities was different. They were confusing and daunting barriers she was uncomfortable facing alone.

When she walked into a hospital, she was forced to confront her mortality. When she walked into a law office, she was forced to confront her vulnerability.

Joseph stood up to greet her with a nod and a smile. In front of his desk was an empty chair. Beside him stood the in-house attorney from Tern Publishing House, Incorporated.

"Shaylee," Joseph introduced, "this is Winston Graves. Winston, Shaylee Simon." They shook hands. His was cool and dry. Hers was sweaty. The look on his slender, non-descript face revealed he'd noticed the moisture. She quickly pulled her hand away.

After taking Joseph's offered seat, she self-consciously wiped damp hands on her lap. Winston occupied a cleared corner of Joseph's desk. His laptop was perched beside a voluminous stack of papers.

Her voice shook as she asked, "Oh, my, is that our contract?"

"Contracts," Mr. Graves corrected. "One is the publishing agreement, the other, a financial agreement."

Her silence, and possibly all the color draining from her face, prompted Joseph to speak. "I've read through these as though they were the bible, Shaylee, the bible" he said through his ready smile. "You'll be very happy with them both."

That smile was doing it, infecting her. The smile she returned was weak with apprehension, but there was affection and trust behind it.

Winston Graves handed them each copies of the contracts. They read through them together, aloud, page by page. Mr. Graves efficiently recited. Joseph readily agreed. Shaylee silently nodded. "There," Joseph soothed after the signings were completed, "that wasn't so bad, was it lass?"

"No," she agreed, "not so bad."

Mr. Graves ceased interaction. He stuffed his own set of the signed contracts into a bulky brown leather satchel. All business and in a hurry, he hoisted his over-filled bag to settle the strap over his left shoulder. He muttered a perfunctory and unbelievable, "It was a pleasure to meet you both," and moved towards the door.

When he'd closed it behind him, Shaylee let out a relieved breath.

Joseph laughed out, "Charming he is not," but she barely heard him. The reality of what had happened rushed up and was beginning to sink in. It was official. She was the sole biographer for James Michael Vincent, and, she would make herself available to work exclusively with Mr. Vincent from August Fourth through September Sixteenth.

## Week One

Shaylee felt a little uneasy showing Jim around her property. She'd grown up poor, living most of her adult life from paycheck to paycheck. But it hadn't made her feel any less guilty about her financial windfall. She didn't need a barn for outdoor parties, or an indoor pool. A smaller, more conservative house would have sufficed.

Jim was gracious, his compliments generous and genuine:

"I can't wait to try out that pool."

"Wow. I wish I had a guest room like this."

"I can't believe how beautiful these views are."

The tour ended in the atrium, just outside the office where they would be spending most of their time. Its roof was greenhouse-style, fashioned simply with pane glass in aluminum framing. The wall separating the office and atrium was free-standing and low, six feet. It was her own design idea, to let in the most natural light. On the opposite side of the office, the wall was floor to ceiling. Centered between built-in oak shelving was a stone fireplace. The outside wall, full of windows, faced west and framed the sunsets for her at the end of every day.

Shaylee showed Jim how to use her landline phone system. His fixed, polite smile trembled as she explained how to retrieve voice mail messages. He kept his answers to silent nods until she was done.

Then came his laughter and, after that, an almost apology. "I'm sorry. I'm sorry, but, but, come on, Shaylee, who uses landlines anymore?" He stared deliberately at her cordless phone. "I mean, come on! Shouldn't this thing be in a museum?"

She smiled because it had made him laugh, but irritation rose when she had to wait for his amusement to die down. She thought she'd waited long enough to ask, "Are you done?" but the question only got him going again.

He was making an effort. The laughter stopped, but the trembling smile stayed on his lips.

"Okay." He inhaled sharply. "Okay." One more deep breath. "I think that's it."

"Are you sure?"

"Yes. I'm sure."

"I use this as my business line," she started, but paused to see if he was going to interrupt again. He did seem to have himself a little more under control, so she continued. "Since I work from home, I need to keep my workspace separate from my personal spaces. It's a mental preparation tool. When I walk into the office, it's work time, and I'm surrounded by work things." She looked around the room and then back to Jim. No more smile. "When I leave the office, I walk away from everything associated with work."

A contrite look crossed his face. He cleared his throat before saying, "Well, now I feel a little foolish. That makes perfect sense."

"So," it was her turn to stare down at the phone, "how much do you think a museum would pay me for this?"

His response was a rich and throaty laugh.

"Sunday never feels like a workday, does it?" Shaylee asked.

"No it doesn't," he agreed. His head shook gently, and tilted to one side. Interest piqued, he waited for her suggestion.

"Would you be interested in a trip to the county fair?"

The Clark County Fair wasn't just a look at country life. It was a blueprint of how to enjoy life in the country. They visited well-cared-for horses, cows, llamas, alpacas, goats, and sheep. In one tin building were chickens, pigeons, and rabbits. In the next building, there were hot tubs and energy-efficient appliances. One more building over were the displays of professional landscapers and building contractors.

Every Grange Hall table was full of freshly picked victory garden samplings. In true country style charm, they were all displayed on a myriad of mismatched plates. Children's drawings, illustrating messages of home and family, had been lovingly placed among them. Outside the hall's open doors were orderly rows of new and used construction and farm equipment.

An "Arts and Crafts" area occupied a third of the air-conditioned events center. On display were handcrafted items submitted by county residents: quilts and needlework, photography, jewelry, paintings, drawings, mixed-media artwork, floral arrangements. All the entries had been awarded ribbons in their categories. They ranged from the top prize of 'Best In Show' to the simple acknowledgment of 'Participant'. Crowded into the rest of the exhibit hall were local and traveling entrepreneurs.

She condensed her tradition of walking every row and seeing every exhibit to spare Jim. Their next destination was the "The Beer Garden." Shaylee never understood the name. There were no flowers. It didn't look like a garden at all, just a tent surrounded by a chain-link fence. But there was plenty of beer. Jim was overwhelmed by the large selection of local micro-brews. With a few well-chosen questions, "Do you like dark beer? Light beer? Ales? Sweet? Bitter?" Shaylee was able to recommend a spice-infused pilsner.

The tent was next to the main grandstand and overlooked its field. The current event was getting underway, an obnoxiously loud demolition derby. They tried to talk over howling engines, screaming fans, and an incessantly shouting announcer, but gave up.

Shaylee let the mellowing effects of the alcohol take over. Her mind wandered to the mechanics behind the show. At the end of the day, workers would scoop up all the dirt and mud with a bulldozer and cart it away in dump trucks. The field would be covered with a layer of bark chips, and the main stage would be re-assembled. By this time tomorrow, a big name (or not so big name) band would be setting up to perform its first show of the day.

She finished her draft within a few gulps of Jim. "Do you want another?"

"No." He wiped some foam off his upper lip and stood up, "but I do want to find something to eat."

Food smells came from every direction. Jim passed by kettle corn, elephant ears, barbequed pork, snow cones, and curly fries. His path lead towards the carnival area food booths. In words and pictures, their signs promised delicious treats. He pointed to one of those signs: Deep-Fried Butter.

What was deep-fried butter? Chunks of cold butter wrapped in pastry dough and cooked in a bath of hot, bubbly oil. Golden brown nuggets were scooped, steaming and fizzing, out of the vat. They were tossed into red and white checkered paper bowls. The finishing touch was a topping of cinnamon sugar and crushed pecans. Shaylee bit into one of them and some of the melted butter gushed into her mouth. Jim laughed while he watched the rest drizzle down her chin. When he took a bite, and the same thing happened, it was her turn to laugh.

Throughout the day, he was sporadically approached by fans. Jim shook every extended hand, answered every question asked of him, and signed his name to every offered piece of paper. While they were enjoying the sights and sounds of the goat barn, a petite young woman approached him. She extended her impossibly tiny hand as though she wanted to shake his. He did not hesitate to raise his hand to meet hers, but neither Shaylee nor Jim expected what happened next. In a motion as swift and as graceful as a snake strike, she brought out a pen, turned his hand palm up, and scrawled her phone number onto it.

As he began to understand what was happening, a blush rose on his face. The color almost matched the bright auburn shade of his brazen fan's dyed hair. When the woman let go, Jim stared at the numbers she'd written on it, as though studying them. His face wore its thin, formal smile and his voice was edged with discomfort. "Thank you?"

It was, apparently, not the reaction she'd expected. She looked up, directly into Jim's eyes, and gave him a practiced smile. He cleared his throat, looked down, then away. The pretty little stranger's smile disappeared, replaced with an ugly scowl. She spun around and stomped away as effectively as anyone could with small feet sporting high heels in six inches of straw.

After she was out of ear-shot, Jim turned to Shaylee and said, "Well, that was embarrassing."

"Yes, it was," she agreed, "for her."

Jim let out an involuntary and nervous laugh. As his smile relaxed, it found its way into his eyes, and then, into his throat. He let out a full, loud, long laugh in appreciation of Shaylee's joke. She joined in, taking the opportunity to enjoy the feeling of shared laughter.

He opened his palm. "I hope this comes out."

She took his hand in hers to study the damage: hastily scrawled numbers in black, medium point felt tip pen.

"Oh, don't worry," her words held a teasing lilt. "A little bleach and some steel wool should take this right off."

Their laughter rose again, and Jim's hand dropped down to his side. He said quietly, "I guess she doesn't know."

"Doesn't know what?"

His eyes widened, then narrowed. He took a long look at her but didn't seem to find what he was searching for.

"Nothing," he shook his head in response to the confused look on her face. His lips pursed. His brow creased, and his eyes continued their search. Deliberately, slowly, he repeated the answer. "Nothing."

A pause in the conversation pulled her focus from Jim to their surroundings. The sounds of carnival barkers and blaring, tinny music put a young girl's smile on her adult lips. Memories led her down the food aisle, past the giant slide, around the house of mirrors, and into the game area. Met with the happy screams of children and the lingering smell of French fries, she and Jim walked the gravel aisles. Rows of oversized stuffed animals dangled overhead, temptingly within reach. A bright orange teddy bear caught Shaylee's attention. It had a sweet, happy face and was almost as tall as she was.

The game looked easy enough: get a single plastic ring over the neck of just one of a sea of milk bottles. Mentally, she picked out a spot for the bear in her office, but her planning was premature. For thirty minutes, they watched each of their tossed rings bounce and skitter, then fall away. Leaving behind the bear she'd already named Marmalade was a sad event, but she knew the perfect place to soothe her disappointment.

Jim looked at the always long line of the Clark County Dairy Women's booth with skepticism. Shaylee assured him, "The line moves quickly, and, the wait will be worth it."

Only twelve short minutes later, they were handed their orders. Hers, a half vanilla, half chocolate soft serve swirl in a sugar cone. His, a generous bowl of peach ice cream, vapors steaming off its melty surface. Jim filled his white plastic spoon and examined it thoughtfully.

His voice teased and his eyes gleamed. "Funny, this doesn't look any different from other ice creams."

The spoon disappeared into his mouth and Shaylee waited for Jim to speak. The haunting wind wood arrangement of a Peruvian quartet added to the suspense. She didn't have to wait long. An expression came to his face, one of bliss, pure cream and sugar bliss.

He smiled and rolled his eyes, trying not to meet her gaze as he admitted, "Okay, I'll have to agree. The best."

Before they left, Shaylee made one last round to collect some of her favorite fair foods. Jim offered to help carry the treats, so she bought more. With both of their arms full, they made the return trip through the hayfield parking lot in search of her car. Scanning the shimmering sea of vehicles, she didn't see a mole hole, tripped, and almost fell. She did manage to right herself, but the foods flew out in all directions.

Jim didn't react at first. Tentatively, he asked, "Was that embarrassing?"

Her reply was laughter. Then, his laugher followed hers. It spread out around them, over fifty sunbaked acres and through the summer air.

Dinner was a celebration of overindulgence mixed with practicality. Deep-fried hamburgers were served with a side of raspberry vinaigrette salad. Shaylee insisted the healthy food would counteract the fatty food, and Jim's mouth was too full to argue.

When their plates were empty, he asked, "Well, what time do we want to get started tomorrow?"

"I don't know. You tell me."

"Well, I'm kind of an early riser, usually up by six, down by ten or eleven."

Shaylee wasn't sure, but thought he might be trying to guess at her schedule because he wanted to fit himself into it. Jim didn't seem the type to rise with the sun, or even need eight hours sleep. Was it a misconception she needed to rethink?

"Well," she started.

Shaylee was usually up by five. Because of a non-existent social life, she would spend her day looking for ways to fill it. The effort was exhausting, and usually ended with her falling into bed before nine. But she was willing to let those little truths stay hidden.

If he was up by six, at her door by seven, seven-thirty? Yes, it would give her enough time to prepare for the waking dream ahead of her - writing a book with one of the most famous people in the world.

"I think," her voice was much calmer than her inner thoughts, "seven-thirty sounds great."

Monday began the tedious task of writing up a complete and detailed outline. Names, dates, and facts. Painstakingly accurate, torturous, names, dates, and facts.

On Tuesday afternoon Shaylee let out a quiet growl before asking Jim, "How does it feel?"

"How does what feel?"

"To be the only person I will ever write an autobiography for?"

Jim laughed. "That bad, huh?"

"Bad? Bad? My mind is screaming."

He laughed again and the screaming calmed to a tolerable whimper.

On Wednesday morning, Jim came to her door with a bouquet of pink daisies in one hand. In the other was a package wrapped neatly in white butcher's paper, the word **Porterhouse** stamped on it. While filling a vase with water, Shaylee asked, "So Jim, since these steaks came with flowers, will I be the one barbecuing them?"

He tried to protest.

"Well, no. Not really. The flowers are an apology-slash-thank-you for all the outline work. And I stopped at the custom meat shop I've been driving by since Sunday."

She already knew the answer, but wanted to hear it directly from him. "Oh, so you're going to cook these steaks?"

"Well, um, you might not want me to do that. Mine always come out raw, or burned, or both."

"You're just completely helpless, aren't you?" she teased.

"Completely," he agreed through a boyish grin.

By end-of-day Friday, both Jim and Shaylee were satisfied with the accuracy of the outline. On Saturday morning, they set out to explore a few of the outdoor markets. First was the Vancouver Farmers Market. It was nice, but small. A drive South, over the I-5 bridge, took them to the Portland Saturday Market.

After a lunch of perfectly seasoned Japanese noodles, they wandered the busy streets looking for dessert. The smell of cinnamon led to a food cart and a shared bowl of warm spiced almonds.

The maze of vendor booths was a lovely backdrop for an unhurried walk and some relaxed small talk. Their voices mixed with others and buzzed in the warm air. Boat horns conversed in the nearby Willamette River. Shaylee enjoyed looking at the displays, but nothing caught her eye. Something did catch Jim's eye, or, more accurately, his ear: a recycled glass wind chime.

"It's not too soft, and not too loud, kind of like your voice," he said while buying it for her.

During the drive home, Shaylee invited Jim to move into her cottage.

"It'll save a lot of driving time, and," she added, "you'll still have your privacy."

"That would be great," he answered immediately, but paused before asking, "but, could it, um, be the guest suite?"

## Week Two

On Sunday, a little after ten a.m., Jim walked through Shaylee's door carrying one of his suitcases. He was wearing a gray sweat suit and a relaxed smile. She hadn't bothered to change out of her comfy pajamas. After he settled in, they listened to music, snacked, watched movies, and ignored all the work they had to do.

After dinner, Shaylee handed Jim a folder, explaining, "I'm pretty tired. I'm going to bed early, but I wanted to give you this before I head downstairs. I had a little time to work up a story sample. Could you read it and let me know what you think in the morning?"

"Already? You've got something finished already?"

"It's not much, just one page."

"Sure. Great. We'll talk in the morning. Good night, Shaylee."

"Good night, Jim."

"Holding Tinsel In My Hands" Excerpt:

*"The neighborhood I knew as a child was a sea of single-family homes that reached the horizon in every direction. Each one of those homes had steps leading from the sidewalk up to a covered front stoop. Every stoop, no matter how small, held at least two chairs. An open invitation to stop, visit, share news, gossip, or a cup of coffee.*

*"After-school street games, interrupted every time a car passed, would slowly shrink as moms called their players in for dinner. On winter days, when we weren't in school, we were shuffled around. Friends' houses, church functions, malls, community centers.*

*"During the summer, the challenge was to stay cool on hot, muggy days until they turned into warm, airless nights. Whenever possible, those sweltering weekends were spent chasing relief at the Jersey Shore or in the Pocono Mountains.*

*"My mother's youngest sister, Nila, lived ten doors away. Her six children, my cousins, were more like brothers and sisters, and she treated*

*us like we were her own. Mostly, that was a good thing, like having an extra mom. Sometimes it was a bad thing, because she disciplined us right along with her kids.*

*"One of the legendary stories we pull out at the holidays is about the day she threatened to put us all into a corner. She tried to carry out her punishment, but there weren't enough corners in the house. She had four kids left over, but with one phone call, the problem was solved. Aunt Nila took my four confused cousins next door. Her neighbor, a long-time friend of the family, happily volunteered her living room.*

*"That was how I grew up; friends and family close by, always feeling loved, protected and included."*

Over breakfast on Monday, Shaylee invited Jim along on her morning walk. It was the only healthy exercise habit she'd ever been able to stick with. It was also a good way to clear her head before a full day of sitting at a desk.

He asked, "Are you going to wear your pajamas on this walk?"

"No, Jim, I'm not."

"You're going to put on some real clothes?"

"Yes, Jim."

"Then, I'm in!"

While they walked, Shaylee wore a smile that wasn't only for Jim, it was because of him. She wasn't sure how he would react to her invitation and was beyond relieved when he so eagerly accepted it. Trying to make it sound like a mere afterthought had not been easy.

What she hadn't confessed was that over the past week, she'd begun to feel strangely close to him. The personal nature of their conversations, the easy flow of creativity between them, the beautiful blur of passing hours. They were drawing her into an intimate relationship with a man she barely knew, but how could she tell him that? What she'd tried carefully not to say was how empty her house felt every time he left it.

Reluctant to bring up the subject of the page she'd given him the night before, Shaylee waited on Jim. The longer he didn't mention it, the more anxious she became. They were almost back to the house before he casually offered, "Oh, and Shaylee, I love what you wrote, just love it."

Relief was strong in her words. "Thank you. I was on pins and needles waiting for you to say something."

He smiled, winked, and whispered, "I know."

She should have been upset, but the little boy grin on his face was one of the most beautiful things she'd ever seen.

Jim followed her into the office, along with the memory of the sun on her skin and the wind in her hair. They sat down to an almost finished outline and went over it together. He pointed out mistakes. She corrected them. Finally, they reached the last section: his family information.

"Let's see. Gillian, named for our Grandmother. She's my oldest sister, ten years older than me. Simon's next, nine years older. Matthew, eight years older. Paul, seven years older. Gabriel, six. No sibling five years older. I'm not sure what happened there. Maybe Mom was sick. Or," he quipped, "maybe Dad was. Mark, four years older. Zachariah, three. Deborah, two, then me. Yes, that's right."

Her lips held a conservative smile, but she barely heard his voice. There was a celebration taking place in her head. 'Yes. It's done. Done, done, done. The outline is done.'

After lunch, they began to write in earnest.

"Being the youngest of nine kids, I always felt like an after-thought, even if I was 'planned.' It wasn't my parents' fault. I was just born into a family that was already full when I got there. They tried to spread their time evenly among all us kids, but that was impossible. There was always something, or someone, that needed their immediate attention. Mark had to get to soccer practice. Gabe wanted them at his football game. Matt needed help with a school project. I don't ever remember seeing Mom sleep. Dad's running joke was that he went to work to get some rest, and he was a construction worker.

"There was never any shortage of drama either. My brother, Paul, found any excuse to complain. It was almost impossible to get a word in edgewise once Deb started in on one of her long-winded tirades. At the dinner table, everyone talked about everything, and all at the same time. I tried, a lot, to get Mom and Dad's attention, but after a while, I gave up. It was easier to stay quiet and keep myself busy.

"In sixth grade, I joined the basketball team. I'd just missed my brother, Zach. He started high school that year. I only had to share middle school with my sister, Deb, but that was enough. She was in eighth grade, popular, and mean. Really, really, mean. Her friends started to notice me when I showed some real talent on the court, and it only infuriated her more. That girl would spit words at me like she hated even wasting them on me. She'd find some little weakness and tease me without mercy.

"Gillian was calmer, sweeter, but she left home to get married when I was ten. And after she left, Deb only got worse. Mom would always say, 'Oh, Jimmy, just ignore her.' Ha! Easier said than done. It's no wonder I felt clumsy and tongue-tied around most of the girls I met.

"Hmmm. Maybe we should tone down the Deb stuff a little. I'm not sure she, or Mom, would appreciate my total honesty on this subject."

Shaylee chuckled as she wrote up the side note. "Making notation: tone down the Deb stuff." They both laughed; a sweet little break in the writing.

"Well, by seventh grade, I was doing pretty good. B-plus average, starter in basketball. Deb had moved on to high school. It kept her busy, and once she got a steady boyfriend, she didn't have near as much time to torture me. I liked being around her when she was with him, too. She was all giggly and compliant, almost happy. I wonder how long it took that poor guy to figure out what a horror she was."

He lowered his head and shook it. "Can you please tone that down too?"

"Toning, toning," Shaylee said as she typed. "How about this? Deb was active in family interactions through the eighth grade. She focused her attentions on outside social activities once she entered high school."

"Wow. You really are amazing," Jim answered through a grateful smile. "Now, where was I? Oh, yes, Sam."

"Samantha was one of the girls in my group of school friends from 'the neighborhood,' one of the kids I grew up with. You know, nothing serious. Just hanging out. I was a little surprised when she started asking me to do stuff outside of school, outside the group. Walk her home, catch a movie, maybe pizza after . . .

"I didn't think much of it until we started high school, but by then, everyone had started pairing off. I think, we both felt pressure to do the same. I know I did. It wasn't only the, 'Oh, poor thing. Can't find anyone.' It was that everyone had to be categorized. No one could just be 'not interested' or 'too busy.' Too many people were eager to fill in the blanks, especially Deb. So, I think, to shut everyone up, that's why I started dating Sam.

"We kissed hello at the school gates every morning. I met her at her locker at the end of last period every afternoon. Sam was sweet and polite. She seemed happy with the social part of our relationship, never pushing for anything more. It was that way all through our freshman year. Not long after tenth grade started, I realized she didn't really care for me. We'd both been going through the motions, and, we'd only been doing it to please other people. I'm pretty sure I did us both a favor when I ended things with her. She treated our break up like she'd treated me. No anger. No yelling. It was all very polite, very," he searched for the right word, "amicable."

"I went through the rest of high school single, filling my time outside of classes with sports, part-time jobs, and, then, acting. I took my first drama class in my second semester of tenth grade, not long after Sam and I broke up. I wasn't really into it at first, just killing time. I was cast in a few small roles but mostly helped with props and backdrops.

"Then, in my junior year, I got the lead in our winter play. Something one of the nuns wrote. It was a re-telling of the story of Joseph, the coat-of-many-colors Joseph, centering around his rise from slavery. I stepped onto the stage in that itchy rag costume, looked out over the audience, and I felt it. I knew, I just knew, acting was what I was meant to do." He paused after hearing his own words and cringed a little.

"But you'll make that sound a little less corny, right Shaylee?"

"Yes, Jim. I'm a wordsmith and a miracle worker."

Laughter, his and hers, filled the empty places in Jim's narratives, and, then, filled the quiet spaces in the rest of the day.

On Tuesday morning, Shaylee and Jim met in the kitchen at the same time. After starting her tea, she poured leftover coffee into the sink and rinsed out the pot.

"Do you want to make your own?" she asked. "I don't drink coffee, so I'm not sure I'm making it the way you like."

"Any way you make it is fine with me."

His additional comment, "I'm not even sure I know how to work one of those things," wasn't very convincing. A little smile played on her lips while she made him a fresh pot.

Jim's stories took her through the end of his senior year, and to the end of the morning. He went silent. Shaylee could almost hear the furious thinking going on inside his head as he planned what to say next.

When he did speak, it was a suggestion. "How about a lunch break, Shaylee. It's almost noon, and I could really go for one of your amazing club sandwiches."

She heard the spice of curiosity in her own voice as she started for him, "And then . . ."

He heard it too, not even trying to hide the pleased look on his face. "And then," his eyes glittered as he spoke, "when we get back to work, you are really going to be earning your pay. I have quite a story to tell you."

Jim took full advantage of the opportunity to prolong Shaylee's obvious anticipation with one tortuous postponement after another.

"After lunch," he promised.

"We didn't take a walk, yet, did we? Let's do that first," was his next excuse.

"Making me wait. For this, you will pay," she tossed the mock threat like a foam ball.

His reply was soft and teasing laughter.

When, finally, they settled in; walk completed, bathroom breaks taken, pillows fluffed, water glasses filled, chairs adjusted; he became quiet again. The room was without his voice for an achingly long time, so, when Jim began to speak, Shaylee was poised to catch every word.

"Right after graduation, I got a full-time job, for the summer. I'd saved up enough from my part-time jobs to buy a car, and fixed it up to do a little racing. Most nights, after work, I drove to the industrial area down under the Walt Whitman Bridge. The place was called Race Road.

"I'd meet up with friends. We'd kill some time, blow off some steam, and challenged anyone that came within earshot to race. Sometimes the cops showed up and we'd all scatter, but it didn't happen much. Most of the time the Philly police were busy. Too busy with real crime to chase after some bored kids burning rubber and racing around on the empty roads.

"One Friday night I got there a little early, to pick a good spot. A lot of people were already there, but others were still showing up. Some of them were there to race. Some of them just wanted to watch. I'd built up a bit of a reputation, winning here and there, enough so I was thought of as a challenge. But that night I was tired; too tired to race. I'd had a rough week, but I didn't want to miss any of the action, so I sat in my car and watched everyone else.

"I think I'd been sitting there for about an hour when, somehow, one of the racers lost control of his car. It jumped the road and hit my car head-on. Gas shot everywhere. I ended up with a puddle of it in my lap and, it was on fire. I was on fire. I knew I was in a lot of trouble, but I couldn't move. I felt the pressure of the steering wheel on my chest. It had me pinned in the seat. I tried to grab it. I wanted to pull it off, or, pull myself free, but the flames were rising up around it. Every time I tried to reach for it, the heat caused my hands to jerk away. I could feel my skin burning. I could smell my skin burning. I tried to call out but I was panicking, hyperventilating, choking on my own voice. I passed out.

"I didn't know until later what happened next, but, when I read the accident report, I found out a police car had pulled up just before the accident and that two officers had seen everything. One of them got my car door open, kicked the steering wheel loose, pulled me out, and put out my burning clothes. His partner helped the kid in the other car. If that hadn't happened, things could have been a lot worse. I don't think a bunch of panicked kids would have been so quick to help.

"I woke up in the hospital two weeks later, coming out of a drug-induced coma. I . . . can't even . . . describe the pain, not in a way that would do it justice. It was . . ."

He exhaled sharply through clenched teeth.

"The shock of that pain could have killed me, and, it might have if I hadn't been so physically fit. They kept me as doped up as they could. I don't remember much of that summer. Just short pictures here and there. Pain everywhere.

"I lost count of all the surgeries, all of the skin grafts. It was six months before I could even stand up. It was a year before I could walk, but only with the help of a walker, and then, a cane. Once the healing had progressed enough, they weaned me off the painkillers. The doctors, the nurses, the physical therapists, everyone tried their best, but withdrawal was still pretty intense. A whole different kind of pain.

"A year and a half later, I started college. Good thing I had insurance on the car. It paid my medical bills, and I ended up with a generous settlement. Not just because of the skin and muscle damage, or the scarring. The burns were deep enough to cause . . . nerve damage. Severe, nerve damage. Permanent, nerve damage to my . . . groin area. The burns, the injuries, they left me, unable to, they left me . . . impotent."

Jim was looking down at the floor, his head in his hands, his elbows balanced on his, she now knew, scarred thighs. It explained why he was always fully clothed, in his show, in his movies. Why, even in the middle of a summer day, he was wearing one of his sweat suits. It also explained his excuses for not using the pool.

"But, believe it or not, I felt pretty lucky. I still do. Because both cars caught fire, the fire department did their own investigation and filed a separate report. In that report, the Fire Chief made some interesting comments. The impact shattered my windshield, but, because I'd left my windows up, the air flowed back out of the front of the car. It suctioned the flames away from my body. Because my windows were closed, there wasn't a cross-draft. Because there wasn't a cross-draft, the flames didn't burn as hot as they could have. And, since the flames didn't burn as hot, my injuries weren't as severe as they could have been. And I only left the windows up because the air was so gritty and dusty that night. I mean, think about it. I might only be alive because I left my car windows up. So, yes, I was lucky. Very, very lucky. The boy, the boy in the other car, he died. He died on the way to the hospital."

Jim paused, maybe a moment of silence, maybe a sign of respect for the dead.

"One of the guys I graduated with, Tom Patrick, was halfway through his sophomore year when I started college, and I was glad he was there.

We hadn't been close, but it meant I wouldn't have to explain my 'situation' to anyone. I knew he'd taken care of that. I was probably his most interesting high school story.

"I wasn't in any shape to try out for the basketball team. I tried to practice when I was feeling up to it, but I didn't get my full strength back until my junior year. Even then, even after I was fully healed, the scarring made it too painful to give any height to my jump. It was so frustrating I gave it up altogether. But, that was okay, because I was able to keep fit by running. Any free time I had, I spent working on my acting skills. I took outside classes and workshops, joined the campus thespian group, even started one of my own.

"Acting became everything to me. It became my passion, my life. It was, in a way, my salvation."

He slowly, deliberately straightened in his chair to look at Shaylee.

"Your comment at the fair?" she asked. "That woman? That's what you meant?"

Jim nodded. "That's what I meant."

"Jim. I didn't know. You understand that, right? I didn't know."

"Yes, Shaylee. I understand that."

She had never followed celebrity gossip. Not on purpose. There might have been a few things she'd learned while skimming a newspaper. She may have accidentally tuned in to the end of a trashy tell-all show, but not that story, not the one Jim had just told her.

At that moment, in that way, must have been how she was meant to learn it. The man, himself, sitting in front of her, his eyes pleading with her to accept the story as he'd offered it: without anger, without sorrow, without pity.

They spent the rest of the day working up a rough draft for that chapter of Jim's book, for that chapter of Jim's life.

On Wednesday morning, he walked into the office and found Shaylee already at the computer. She invited him to use the pool with the explanation, "I think I should work on this alone for a while. Is that okay?"

The look he gave her was questioning, and it bordered on suspicion, but he agreed.

Jim had been working with her long enough to see her hesitate, second-guess, and back-step. She didn't want him to see the effort it would take for her writing to show proper respect to his experience. She didn't want him to see that she would need to take on his suffering before she could accurately describe it.

She lost track of the hours. One day was gone. Then, two. Her world became the computer screen. Its flat, square eye illuminated her, stared at her, and stared into her. It saw her ideas spill together, hold ground, and fall apart, only to find their way again. It was the only audience to her own personal drama, and it watched as she fought to build the story up in front of her.

Jim was temporarily banned from the office. The only times she left it was when she had questions or for tea or food breaks. During their meals, she tried to keep him engaged in small talk, and away from the subject of her writing. By Thursday evening his impatience was obvious. He'd let his growing frustration take over their conversations.

"It's still not ready?" he asked, for the third time, during dinner.

Her answer was a coy, "Is this your version of, 'Are we there yet?'"

His response was a stony glare.

By the end of Friday afternoon, everything that had been in her head was in writing. Jim had hunkered down in the small sitting area off the kitchen. Every time she came out, there was another glass, another dish, another magazine, filling the available flat surfaces in the nook. They stacked up higher and higher around him until the clutter looked like a miniature landscape. The tense way he perched in the recliner, his unflinching stare. At just the right angle, he looked like a movie monster wading through downtown Tokyo.

Jim claimed to be passing the time by watching TV, but, his suite had its own entertainment center. It was more likely he'd chosen that spot so he could easily be seen, and heard, from the kitchen.

His temperament didn't change, but, she had to admit, his questions got more creative:

"Patient out of surgery yet?"

"Are these the times that try men's souls?"

"So, how far along are you?"

Dinner time brought Shaylee out of the office and straight into Jim's bothered attitude. Chatting cheerfully while she prepared savory chicken fried rice didn't lighten his mood, or hers. As they ate, she stole a few covert glances. How could he so effectively chew and hold such a dour expression on his face? Impressive.

Maybe his favorite dessert, crepes, would ease the tension. She explained the ingredients she was using in a French, high-pitched, old lady accent.

"We whisk the eggs gingerly into the milk, drizzle in the oil, mix in the flour a bit at a time so that there are no lumps. See," she held out the bowl for him to look, "no lumps. A dash of salt. A dash of sugar, and my own secret flavoring, a whisper of lemon zest."

His scowl was still intact.

"The cherry sauce is a combination of some perfectly lovely things. Fresh frozen sweet Bing cherries picked from my own tree just two weeks ago, cream, sugar, a dash of vanilla, and a soupçon of red wine."

The silence behind her was louder than the simmering burgundy sauce in front of her. Annoyance leaked into the narrative.

"And now, we drizzle the aromatic sauce generously over the crepes. Voilà."

She turned to him and dropped the accent. In a calm, low voice, she warned, "Jim, if I don't see a smile on your face, I promise you, I will dump this in the trash."

His eyes widened. His lips pursed, then set into a straight, thin line. She held the plate in front of him, just out of reach.

"Threats," he grumbled. "Really? Threats? You're holding my food hostage?"

"Your food? No, not your food. My food. It's my food. And I decide if you get it. I decide if you are deserving. So, Jim, are you? Deserving? Well, are you?"

Shaylee offered one of her smiles as an example and received a grudging smirk with a dry, one-syllable chuckle.

"Close enough," she conceded, her attention focused on setting the plate in front of him without meeting his humorless gaze.

While Jim ate, Shaylee cleaned the kitchen, hoping he wouldn't notice her painfully slow pace, or see it for what it was: an obvious attempt to avoid talking to him, or, looking at him. The subtle clinking sounds of fork to plate subsided as she filled the dishwasher.

In a tone that left no opening for contradiction, she announced to the sink, "Remember Jim, I won't be up at my usual time tomorrow. I'm going to stay up late to work on the chapter."

He took a deep, ragged breath, grumbling out, "Yes Shaylee, I remember," and marched away.

The bedroom door closed with enough force to test the hinges. As the dishwasher door closed with a satisfyingly noisy thunk, a smile came to her face. A muffled giggle leaked from that smile. A careful glance to make sure he hadn't reemerged, and she let loose full-on laughter.

She'd done it, found the positive, and Jim wasn't even aware of what he was doing. He was showing her a different side of the man who'd introduced himself to her a month ago. How easily he'd transformed. The smiling companion relaxing into the atmosphere around him disappeared. The focused professional, picking, digging, and pushing to expose what he wanted entered. And, in true Jim style, it was a strong, palpable approach, but without pretense or aggression.

The giddy discovery brought with it a wave of calming, too. Unexplained edginess was her subconscious whispering a reminder: this is why you and Jim are together.

The situation had distracted her from her priority: to observe. She'd forgotten to take that one step back and study him with a writer's eyes. Shaylee ripped open the secret with the gusto of a toddler tearing at a package of cookies, and was enjoying the spoils. How delicious, how energizing, this riddle she'd solved.

Moving was effortless. The kitchen almost cleaned itself. She floated into the office and perched lightly in her chair. With keyboard caresses, she coaxed the mood from her mind to her fingers and into the almost finished chapter.

When it hurt to blink, she staggered to bed and turned the alarm off, not caring that Jim would have only an empty coffee pot to complain to in the morning.

A little after ten a.m. her eyes opened. She stretched, slowly, fully, appreciatively, into the soft warmth around her. Faint bird calls from the forest touched the quiet of the room, encouragement to get up and be a part of the day.

Her morning might have started late, but it was already in full swing when she walked into the kitchen. There was Jim, sitting at the dining room table, his coffee cup empty, his attitude full.

The inquisition started with, "Did you finish it yet, Shaylee? Did you finish the chapter?" and was delivered through a deeply creased frown.

She'd planned to offer him a knowing smile and a graciously understanding nod, but his surly attitude chased away her self-promised calm. Unintentionally, her face took on a puckered glare of its own.

"What?" he asked innocently. When her expression didn't soften, he looked down and cleared his throat, restlessly testing the confines of his chair. She immediately regretted her response, her completely reasonable and not at all overdramatized response. That irritated her more.

Between the brewing of coffee and the serving of scrambled eggs, Jim's earlier discomfort was forgotten. He slipped back into his dogged bent. The unending questions continued, until she found herself commiserating with the lemon she'd zested the night before.

"You've got to be finished by now. You've got to."

"No, Jim, not yet. Almost, but not quite yet."

He raised his left arm and commented to his wristwatch. "Hey, Shaylee, in ten minutes it will officially be," then looked up at her, "for-ev-er."

She turned away from him and the out-of-patience expression he'd etched onto his face. Determined steps took her towards the atrium. Walking lightly, she listened for following sounds behind her. There were none.

After closing the office door, she sat down to face the completed chapter in front of her. Just after two-thirty, and her fourth read-through, the final edits were made. Every word was carefully chosen. Every sentence was descriptively perfect. Every phrase was meticulously crafted, and, ready for Jim.

As he sat down at the computer, she made it clear she was giving him privacy. "Please, Jim, take your time. Take all the time you want. I'll be in the kitchen."

He needed to take it in at his own pace, without the feeling of being pressured or hurried. He needed to be left alone with the story and his own thoughts. Once he fully understood what she'd written, he was going to realize she'd given him a part of herself as a gift. He would need time to decide how he was going to accept it.

On her way out of the office, she closed the door, relieved to be on the other side of it. The mission complete, the challenge met, the weight of the past four days began to lift. Out of the house and onto the deck, Shaylee felt stopped time resume. Her favorite lounge chair was waiting for her, the light layer of dust a teasing reminder she'd been away. As she sank into it, the cushions hissed with her weight, exhaling along with her.

Overhead was a sky thick with clouds. They'd blocked the sun for most of the day, so the air was cool. A mild summer day: the perfect opportunity to do some baking.

For Shaylee, baking had always been a kind of therapy. A way to slow down runaway days. A way to forget things her mind nagged her to remember. Bringing random ingredients together to make something completely different was her way of getting lost in the moment. The only meaning of time was to calculate doneness. The most complex questions she needed to ask herself were, "Should I add sage to that?" or "Where's the big bowl?" Every other thought could be pushed away by the music of the electric mixer, or lost in the act of scraping batter into an oven-bound pan.

She took in a deep breath infused with herbs and spices. The counter was covered with cooling baked goods: four dozen biscuits, six loaves of quick bread. And, it was five o'clock. Crispy pork chops would complement the still-steaming cheddar and rosemary biscuits.

Her head in the fridge, she was noisily searching the crisper for salad fixings. But, because she'd been listening for him, she heard Jim walk up behind her.

Shaylee didn't straighten up right away. She'd learned a lot about Jim over the past weeks. He'd shared the most private details of his life over the past days, but he still wasn't much more than an acquaintance. He might be angry she'd taken creative liberties in telling his story. He might be disappointed in what she'd written. She might think she'd come to know him, but had no idea what to expect.

At first, he seemed to be in shock. His face was frozen. At first, when she looked into his eyes, he didn't look back. She could only imagine what was going through his mind. She'd had days to create, and refine, the chapter. Jim had spent only a few hours with it.

Thinking through what to say before she said it, Shaylee practiced the words in her head. She wanted them to come as lightly as possible.

"You were in there a long time, Jim. How many times did you read the chapter?"

He didn't answer. She took the opportunity to set the collection of vegetables on the counter.

"Jim?"

His words were deep and hushed.

"Five times, Shaylee. I read it five times."

She was eager to hear his opinion, but only heard silence. The lettuce, cucumber, tomato, and radishes were an immediate outlet for her frustration. Over the sounds of chopping, over her shoulder, she commented casually, "I hope it was worth the wait."

No response.

Thinking of another approach, she set down her knife and turned to face him.

"Are, are you happy with it?"

He nodded.

"Did I explain your feelings in the right way, Jim?"

He nodded.

"Did I leave anything out?"

He shook his head.

"Did I do a good job describing how you've accepted things, how you've come to terms with your, with your, loss?"

He nodded.

"And your attitude? Did I express your attitude in the right way, Jim?"

In a throaty whisper, he answered. "Yes, Shaylee. You said it perfectly. You said it all, you said everything, perfectly. I had no idea what to expect, but. . ."

Within the next words, he found his voice. "To see that part of my life in writing was one thing, but then, then, the way you wrote it."

She saw his eyes come to life, saw the emotions run in and out of them. Those eyes, those steel-blue eyes, showed her everything: his appreciation, his admiration, his gratitude.

"It's as if, as if you took everything I said, and put it in your heart before you wrote it down."

She took a deep breath, relieved he'd accepted the gift as graciously as she'd offered it.

¤ ¤ ¤ ¤ ¤ ¤ ¤ ¤ ¤ ¤ ¤ ¤ ¤

Shaylee had been trying to impress Jim with various culinary adventures, but Sunday evening was not one of those times. They looked down over the remains of a failed quiche. He laughed out the words, "It looks like you scrambled it up in a frying pan!"

Not ready to enjoy the joke, she voiced a stern, "Don't give me any ideas."

All evidence of the offending meal was removed from the counter. A satisfied smirk came to her lips as the garbage disposal swallowed every bit of the runny yellow goo. Looking up, she caught Jim in a thoughtful gaze. He quickly turned away, letting out one of his nervous little laughs.

As she cleaned out the pan, she wondered what had him so deep in thought. His entire attitude towards her had changed since yesterday, since he'd read the accident chapter. There was something he was feeling, something he was trying to keep private, but couldn't quite hide. Something as subtle as the movement of a flower trying to face the sun.

In the back of the freezer was a stash of frozen dinners. She usually raided it when she was too tired, or too lazy, to cook. It also came in handy for failed-food-experiment emergencies. A family-sized lasagna. Perfect. It would pair well with the nutmeg spiced grape salad she'd already made.

Dinner conversation centered around why they were eating from the freezer. The sting of failure was still fresh, but she couldn't stop herself from laughing at Jim's comment. "I swear, that thing was looking back at us."

With the meal finished, she began to clear the table. Still, he was watching her. In his eyes were hints of a question. She wondered what it might be. She wondered when, or even if, he would ask it.

The sun disappeared behind the trees, a signal to let the day come to its natural ending. Jim's small talk while she did the dishes. Quiet good nights. Promises to meet again in the morning.

## Week Three

Their progress was steady but leisurely. Time passed in a seamless blend of creativity, laughter, and rest. Mornings found Shaylee impatient to shake off sleep, eager to put the new day on with her summer clothes.

She described her feelings of job satisfaction with synonyms like engaging, satisfying, rewarding. And Jim? How many times had he smiled and said how nice it was to get a break from Hollywood?

But sometimes, they did find themselves off-topic. He asked about some of her other works in progress. She brought a folder of current writing projects up onto the computer screen. Searching a document list, she said haltingly, "I've got a few finished short stories."

"Really?" Jim exclaimed. "Have anything handy? I think I've talked about myself enough for one day."

"I'm not sure I believe that," she bantered. "A man tired of talking about himself?"

An over-played look of pain crossed his face. "That's what you think of me? I'm hurt." He pouted angelically, adding, "You're not wrong, but still, I'm hurt."

When they both started to giggle, she agreed it was time for a break.

"Okay." She opened one of her files. "Here's one. The back-story is simple. Jon, seventeen, is fifteen-year-old Rachel's first lover. They spend the summer together. Summer turns to autumn. Rachel is experiencing changes in her body. Changes in her attitude towards herself, towards her surroundings, towards Jon."

She read aloud.

## The Story

"Rachel made her way along the road, the road she loved to walk on rainy nights. She stopped at the old apple tree, a tree everyone called magic. Anyone sitting under it for even a short time became confused, light-headed, and euphoric. The tree was next to a wetland field. During winter white-outs, that field became *the* spot to gather. Elaborate snow fortresses, snowball wars, sledding, four-wheeling, ice skating. They could all happen together in one open, uninterrupted space.

"At the edge of that field was 'The Barn.' Even if she tried, she could never count up the hours she'd spent in that weathered gray building. Friends and neighbors built intricate mazes out of straw and hay bales. Those mazes disappeared when someone's horses or cows needed to be fed, and were repaired or re-created after every disturbance. It had been their meeting place, their clubhouse, their haven, and, their secret. Other than the owner occasionally filling or emptying it, that barn had been left to them.

"Everything somehow related to everything else in the familiar flow of Rachel's day-to-day life. When she was a child, she would walk to the edges of that world, stop, look as far as the skyline, but go no farther.

"As she grew older, those boundaries became a starting point. She would take a few steps further out each time she reached them. Then, spend more and more time outside of them before making her way back in. There was an excitement in leaving, a comfort in returning. She could wander off in any direction, into any adventure. And, when it was time to return, there would be a clear path waiting for her. She knew that one landmark would lead to another. That the threads running between them, connecting them, would always lead the way home.

"Her thoughts were interrupted with Jon's, 'Let's go inside,' as he walked out of the night towards her. There was an obvious urgency in his voice. Rachel smiled, knowing she was the reason for that urgency. They walked into the barn together and her childhood retreated into the corners.

"It had been almost a month since he'd last called her. Even after his long absence, she still couldn't stop herself from running to him. She'd known, almost from the beginning, he wouldn't be faithful. It had bothered her, at first, but not for long. There was no shortage of young men who wanted to spend time with her; attractive, sweet, attentive young men. Finding companionship was never a problem, but there was still a special place in her heart for her first lover. She felt that place fill with his words, with his touch.

"The night was clear; the moon, half full. Light found its way through the cracks in the barn's aging roof and walls, striping everything in silver. The sweet smell of dried hay was strong enough to taste. She breathed it in while taking off her shoes. Jon took his off too. Their movements stirred the coarse, dried grasses underfoot, and the scent rose stronger.

"He tried to kiss her, but she stepped away from him, out of his arms. 'Wait, she whispered, 'let me.'

"As she took his shirt off, she kissed the skin where the fabric had just touched him. That fabric, and her kisses, spilled off his shoulder, down his chest. She knelt, pulled down his pants and underwear, then stood up and backed away to let him finish undressing. Naked, he stepped towards her. There was raw desire in his eyes and he was aroused, fully aroused.

"She felt herself blush when he began to unbutton her blouse. Light kisses tickled her neck as her shirt fell to the floor. He took off her bra, catching his breath when her small, newly formed breasts were freed. Jon took them in his hands, kissing each one before letting his lips stray down to her pant line. He licked and kissed around her navel, unbuttoning her jeans as he did. She stepped out of them and they joined the rest of the clothes on the floor. Jon cupped her buttocks and let his hands slide down the back of her legs. He got onto his knees and kissed each of her ankles, first on the outside, then the inside. Her gaze was intent as she watched him spread their clothing out into a patchwork blanket.

"Jon laid down on them and reached out for her in the semi-darkness. She took his hand and let him guide her down to lay beside him. He rose above her, entered her. Every sensation in her body was directed to the parts of him that were touching her. All she could feel was him moving inside of her, his skin gliding over hers.

"It didn't even seem that he was perched over her. It was as though he had fallen into her, that when he moved, she moved, that he breathed in the air she was exhaling.

"So caught up in the moment, so caught up in the act of their lovemaking, she was surprised when it happened. The first touches of pleasure reaching out from inside her. They fell. They rose, grew stronger, spread out. Leisurely, they pulsed through her veins like thick honey.

"Freed by her own moans, the sensation found its way to every part of her body. Her bones were liquid. Her skin was velvet. There was no barn, no floor, no time; only Jon gently caressing her every nerve.

"He cried out and scooped Rachel even closer to him. His heart pounded against her chest. His panting filled her ears. Her eyes fell closed so that vision couldn't distract her from what she was feeling. Her body retelling the story of her first orgasm.

"Jon was smiling when Rachel opened her eyes. She was smiling when she reached up to stroke the side of his face. His smile disappeared into hers, into a kiss."

Heat rose in her face. She hadn't thought ahead when picking the story, realizing too late how inappropriate it was. Turning to him with the intent of apologizing, embarrassment dropped her eyes. She quickly looked down and away, but not before catching a glimpse of, his crotch.

In the time it took to blink, she turned away, but turned back, and then, couldn't stop staring. There it was; a shape, a familiar shape. Under even his loose-fitting sweat pants, there was an unmistakable outline.

A confused look played on Jim's face, until his gaze followed hers. His eyes widened. His expression froze as he began to understand what had happened, what she was seeing.

Jim stood up and said quietly to the ceiling, "I think I need a break." As he spoke, he covered the distance from the chair to the door. Astonishment froze Shaylee in her chair. She watched him leave, heard him close his bedroom door, felt his absence. Unable to move, she could only sit, and stare, and wonder.

¤¤¤¤¤¤¤¤¤¤¤¤¤¤

Mixing together a strawberry, blueberry, and romaine lettuce salad, Shaylee tried to decide on dinner. What type of meat went best with lies? Was there an appropriate side-dish to serve with discovered secrets? Steak and baked potatoes seemed a suitable choice - deceptively simple.

She made up a plate for Jim and carried it to his door.

A blurted "Dinner's ready," startled her, too loud for the quiet hallway. In a softer voice, she continued.

"I'm just going to leave it here. On the table. Outside the door. You like your steak medium, right? Okay then. Good night."

By the time Shaylee'd stopped talking, she felt awkward, and, it was a good guess she'd made Jim feel the same way.

The plate she'd made up for herself went with her downstairs, to her room. As she ate, she tried not to think, but that was impossible. She was angry at him for lying, but sorry the incident had even happened. She wanted to go to Jim and accuse him. She wanted to go to Jim and comfort him. But, mostly, she wanted to know the reason behind his story, a story he'd led the world to believe.


Shaylee spent the night in and out of sleep, in and out of remembering. Her eyes opened to the day's first pale gold light and she went upstairs to the kitchen. A pot of coffee started, she filled a teacup with water and set it in the microwave. It circled again and again, the same way questions moved around her mind. The water boiled up and over the sides. She wiped up the spill, prepared her tea, and took it out onto the deck. There was one lone cloud stretched over the eastern horizon, a bright streak. It looked like a gash that had been cut in the sky for the sun to rise through.

Out of the corner of her eye, she caught Jim's movements in the kitchen. Through the window, she watched him put his plate in the sink and pull a mug out of the cupboard. He stood in front of the coffee maker, waiting for it to finish brewing. Her eyes held their focus on him as he filled his cup. He walked out of the kitchen, through the living room, out the door, towards her. Shaylee's whole body tensed when he looked at the chair across from her. Relief unclenched her neck and shoulders when he chose the seat beside her. She took a sip of tea, and let her gaze wander out over the lawn.

"You have questions," he stated, not even bothering to form a question.

It took a few deep breaths and a lot of self-restraint to answer a calm and simple, "Yes."

"Shaylee, I . . . I," he began, then stopped.

"Shaylee," he began again, "I, I want to answer your questions. I do. I want to tell you, everything. When we met, we hit it off right away, didn't we? You're so easy to talk to. It feels like I've known you forever, like I can be completely honest with you, like I can tell you everything I'm feeling, like everything I say is, is safe with you. You seem to know, you seem to understand . . . "

His voice faded. She wasn't sure if he was waiting for a response, or just trying to remember how to form a complete sentence. This time, she knew why he was so nervous, and stayed silent.

"I don't know how to start," he said, and then, true to his words, didn't seem able to continue.

He cleared his throat and opened his mouth. Nothing. He cleared his throat again.

Morning continued on around them. The sun rose higher. The air began to warm. The flowers opened wider, and, she was sure she saw the grass grow a little.

"Jim," she intervened, "as far as I'm concerned, we can pretend yesterday didn't happen. Last night's story can end with, 'We finished writing for the day, had a nice dinner, and then called it a night.'"

He sounded surprised. "Is that what you want?"

"What I want," she felt her voice catch, "is for this morning to be like all the others since you got here. I want you to finish your coffee and ask me what's for breakfast. I want you to only be half-listening when I tell you, because we both know you'll eat whatever I put in front of you. I want you to tell me to get out of my pajamas and into some real clothes because, 'It's time to start the day.' I want, I want . . . " she tried to finish, but lost her words when she turned to look at him.

His face was in profile, the muscles in his jaw and neck taut. There was no need to look into his eyes to know they were intense with emotion. What she wanted to believe was that things would go back to "normal," but it was obvious he was not going to ignore what had happened. There was something he was preparing himself to tell her, and, when he'd had his say, he was going to ask the question she'd seen in his eyes. For the first time since they'd met, she was afraid of what he was going to say next.

Shaylee's voice was weak. "I've told you what I want." Her next words came out as a whisper. "What do you want?"

Then, she let her silence settle between them.

Jim stood up, moved into the chair across from her, and set his mug down on the table in front of him. His hands cupped around it. He looked down into it, and then, set it aside. When he raised his head, she looked into his eyes, his frightened, but determined, steel-blue eyes.

"I told you about me and Samantha," Jim said, "about our break-up, but I didn't tell you the whole story."

His words rushed over themselves. Was he was afraid that if he stopped, he wouldn't be able to continue?

"One evening, we found ourselves alone at her house. We'd finished dinner and homework and were just watching TV in the family room. Her brothers and sisters all left the house with one excuse or another. I got up to get a drink and saw her parents leaving."

"I asked Sam, 'Where are your parents going?'"

"'There's a parent-teacher meeting at school,' she answered.

"I got a soda and settled in on the couch. Neither one of us initiated it. We locked eyes, moved towards each other, and, started kissing. It was," he swallowed hard and gasped out the word, "amazing."

"She was so, soft, so warm, silky. I wanted, more. Pretty soon, I was taking off her shirt, her bra. She didn't stop me. My hands started to shake, so she helped me take off my shirt."

He sighed, the past in his eyes. Memories slowed and thickened his words.

"We were lying down on the couch, side by side, kissing. The feeling of our bodies rubbing against each other. The look of curiosity on her pretty face. The look of, expectation, in her eyes. I took off her pants, her underwear, and then mine. We began to touch, to explore. She took my penis in her hand, but, nothing happened. She waited for a while, but still, nothing. I took her into my arms, and we kissed some more, but . . . "

He shook his head. She could almost feel the pleasure turn to pain inside him.

"She pulled out of my arms. She pulled away from me. She grabbed her clothes and ran out of the room. I, I, I'd never felt so many things at the same time in my life. I couldn't make any sense, any sense, out of any of it. I picked up my clothes. I got dressed. I left."

His words held that pain out to Shaylee, offering it to her.

"The next morning, I waited for Samantha in front of the school, but she didn't show up. I didn't see her once that day. At first, I thought, 'Maybe this is something we can work out.' After last bell, I waited at her locker, alone. I was sad, scared, confused, upset. On the walk home, alone, I started to get the feeling nothing was going to be worked out.

"We really had just been polite strangers. That was probably *why* nothing happened. I'd never thought of her in that way. Our relationship hadn't been much more than two conveniently-located people spending time together. Our conversations were all just superficial small talk. By the time I walked through the door, I was even feeling a little relieved. I could stop pretending, you know, stop putting on a show for everyone.

"Well, I hadn't even made it to my room before Deb came barreling down the hallway at me, laughing.

"'Jimmy, is it true? You gotta tell me. I can't stand it. I just can't stand it! Tell me you didn't do an impression of the incredible shrinking boy at Sam's last night.'

"She'd barely taken a breath when she grabbed my face and forced me to look into her eyes. I pulled away from her.

"She screeched, 'It's true. It's true.'

"Her cackling followed me into my room. I could still hear it through the closed door. I could still hear it through my hands over my ears."

"The rollercoaster ride I experienced after that. Sam's betrayal was one thing, but, the next day, at school. The whispers and laughter that followed me out of every room. Loud conversations that stopped abruptly when I came into view. Outright mocking and cat-calls. I kept my mouth shut and my eyes down, and, I never looked Samantha in the eye again. I concentrated on my school work, spent longer hours at basketball practice, longer hours at my jobs. I ran myself ragged every day, hoping I could just fall into an exhausted sleep every night.

"Things eventually calmed down. But, still . . ."

Jim watched her intensely as he spoke, making her even more aware of the emotions that crossed her face. Empathy, understanding, barely contained sympathetic anger. She was having trouble keeping her chin from quivering. He saw that too.

"Through the rest of high school, I didn't pursue another girl. And none of them showed any interest in me. But acting, acting became my love. Acting became my outlet. I could say what I wanted, do what I felt. They weren't my words or my actions. They were only parts I played. I could pour my soul out onto the stage, and then, just walk away. No embarrassment. No shame. No consequences.

"The accident, it was a well-timed coincidence. I took the opportunity to "embellish" the extent of my injuries. It gave people a real reason to pity me, and, it gave me a real reason to avoid dating. It did a great job of swallowing up the 'Samantha' story, too. How could anyone even think it was funny after everything poor Jimmy had gone through?"

He forced out a bitter chuckle.

"Even Deb's attitude towards me changed after that. She was suddenly the concerned sister.

"Mom and Dad had to make my medical decisions while I was in the coma, and during that first summer I was on all those pain killers. But, after that, I started making my own decisions. I'd just turned eighteen, and, because I'd been paying my own insurance premiums, my family didn't have any more access to my medical records. They only knew what I told them. The only people who knew the truth were bound by confidentiality laws. None of my doctors, nurses, physical therapists, none of the medical staffers, were allowed to share that information with anyone.

"My insurance company paid all the bills, and even my copies of those bills went directly to a law firm. My lawyer, he was able to settle my claim out-of-court. We didn't have to file a legal action, so my case never became a matter of public record.

"I got a fair damages settlement: medical bills, lost wages, the car's value, pain and suffering. I do have some permanent injuries. There's deep scarring and numbness on both of my thighs, and, because of the scars, I still have pain when I jump, or when I lift something too heavy.

"The settlement was big enough to convince everyone I'd received a huge pile of money for my other permanent damage, for my, supposed impotence. I just secretly started racking up my student loan debt. They never knew any better. And that lie didn't come back to bite me, thanks to all the money I made in Hollywood."

Then, he stopped talking. Then, it was his silence between them.

Shaylee looked, carefully looked, at Jim. She saw a sensitive, confused, hurt teenage boy. She saw a shy young adult unable to come to terms with his past, or his pain. She saw the myth, the stranger who'd dropped himself down into the middle of her life a month ago. She saw the sweet, charming companion who'd been filling her days with stories and laughter. And, she saw, in front of her, at that moment, a man facing his own fear, a fear so strong it was a physical presence.

She spoke to all of them.

"Jim, I can only imagine what you've been through, but I don't have to imagine what it did to you. I can see it in your eyes. I can hear it in your voice."

There was one thing she did had trouble imagining. There was one thing she had to ask him, just to be clear. "You, you never met anyone? You never had a relationship?"

"No." He shook his head, but his eyes never left hers.

She asked him in a different way, just to make sure. "You never met a woman who . . ."

She stopped, and started again. "You never . . ." Her voice trailed off as her head tilted slightly.

He said again, slowly, his voice softer, deeper, "No."

Jim reached over the table and took one of her hands into his. But he wasn't merely holding her hand. Every part of him was facing her, watching. Every part of him was attuned to her, waiting.

The look on his face . . . innocent desire.

There had been times she'd felt alone, all alone, even in a crowd of thousands. There had been times she'd felt like there wasn't any air to breathe in a room with only one other person in it. But she'd never felt what Jim made her feel: like she was alone with the only other person on Earth.

And that feeling was the only thing she was sure about. Everything else was unknown. Everything else was partial questions. They ran through her, crashed together, and then shot out in different directions.

"I'm not sure. Jim. I'm just not sure. I'm confused. So . . . confused."

Jim broke their gaze, pulled away, and stood up. He turned, poised to walk away.

She stopped herself from reaching out to him. Her touch could hurt more than help. His touch would confuse her more.

Gently, as gently as she possibly could, she said, "Stop, Jim. Please. Stop."

He did stop, and turned to Shaylee again.

The look on her face must have been the right combination of pleading and compassion. He took a deep breath, and his body settled into the place he was standing.

She didn't think about what to say, she just started to talk.

"This is a lot, Jim. You have to admit it. This is a lot, to take in."

He nodded in agreement, the look of a hurt child on his face, the fear of a man in his eyes.

She went on. "One minute we're strangers. The next we're long lost friends, sharing the summer. And now, and now, y-you want me to look at you, to, to see you, in an entirely different way. You want me to treat you in an entirely different way."

Involuntarily, her voice deepened. "I'm not saying no. I'm just saying, I need some time. Please, Jim, just a little time."

He nodded again and closed his eyes. When they opened, the hurt look was gone, and his fear seemed a little more under control. Jim stepped towards her and reached out . . . for his coffee cup. He picked it up and looked down into it, at his cold coffee.

It took some time for him to compose himself before he looked up at her and asked, "Well, then, what's for breakfast?"

It took some time for her legs to stop shaking before she stood up and answered, "How about an omelet?"


Shaylee replayed Jim's newest story in her head; once, twice, a third time. How many times before it became real? What he wanted, that didn't seem real either. Jim was no fumbling man-child, no painfully shy introvert holed up in his mother's basement. He was something even she could never have imagined.

After breakfast, they took a walk, as they usually did. What was unusual was that they were quiet the whole time. Their walk finished, they entered the office together. They wrote, discussed details, made changes that led to more discussions and more details. What was unusual? When Jim wasn't concentrating on their work, he was concentrating on her. And the question in his eyes? It wasn't a hint anymore.

Six o'clock came, and when it did, they ate dinner. During their meal, the sun fell behind the trees. When the shadows of the trees reached over the house, the house, as usual, began to cool. The darkness came at its expected time, but there was nothing routine about that night. On that night, their voices were hushed. Their eyes were intent. They talked about usual things, but those words did not have the same meaning.

At nine o'clock, they said at their usual good nights, but even those familiar words sounded different. There was something new in the space between them, something waiting to find its own words.

It was early, still dark, when she passed his door, his open door, and went to the kitchen. While her tea steeped, she made coffee. It had just finished brewing when he came to her. Shaylee filled a cup and offered it to him. He set it on the counter and took her hands in his, guiding her arms around his waist. His arms wrapped around her. His heat, his scent, surrounded her too.

Their first kiss was simple. It was sweet. It was chaste, and, it was only the first. The next was longer, but hesitant. He paused, an invitation for her to intervene? She opened her mouth slightly and let her tongue explore the inside of his mouth. He did the same. Like a sensual game of 'Simon Says', he matched her, touch for touch, kiss for kiss.

His breathing became heavier. She took his hands in hers and placed them over her breasts. Even through the fabric of her robe, even through her bra, she felt them respond to his touch. She felt herself respond to his touch. Her breathing became heavier.

To his room, to the edge of the bed. Off came his sweatshirt. Her kisses and touches made their way down his chest. As she pulled his pants down, she nudged him until he sat on the edge of the bed. More kisses. More touching. Jim's pants fell to the floor. Freed of his clothes, they stood up together, and the game continued . . .

Shaylee introduced Jim to a new part of himself. An awakening sexual creature with the appetite of a starved man. He wanted to try everything. Any idea they shared was acted on. Any whim was entertained. Any question he asked, she answered, sometimes, with no words at all. His uninhibited eagerness, his curiosity, his ingenuous wonder. They were, in themselves, new experiences for her.

A whispered question, "What would it be like to walk barefoot on the beach with you?" was answered within hours.

The sun was setting on Seaside, Oregon. They found themselves alone in the dunes and lost in a kiss. Jim, being a gentleman, laid down before pulling Shaylee on top of him, so she wouldn't have to suffer the scratching sand on her delicate skin. Shaylee, being a lady, tried not to kick up too much of that sand once her delicate skin found his.

# Week Four

On Tuesday, they took another trip, north. Jim said they had to hike Mount Rainer together, because she'd never done it. During that leisurely and flirty adventure, they wandered into a secluded canyon. A glacial stream ran through it. The quick-moving water was ice cold, bubbly, and tasted like melted snow. Along the shaded bank of the stream was a smooth-worn boulder covered with moss. It was large enough and flat enough and soft enough to lay on, so they did.

From the base of Mt. Rainer to the outskirts of Seattle, the drive was over an hour. A fifty-five-minute crawl through sluggish city traffic brought them to the Pike Place Market. A dinner of surf and turf became a sensual feast when Shaylee dipped a piece of lobster tail in butter, placed it gingerly on a thin slice of steak and fed it to Jim. His eyes flashed their pleasure. Her smile glowed in return. Their public table may well have been a private booth in an intimate restaurant. They touched, held hands, kissed over the table, and shared promises of how delicious dessert was going to be. On their walk to the car, they held hands.

The street was still clogged with stop-and-start traffic. The air was unmoving, dusty, and thick with exhaust fumes. How long would it take to get to a good hotel? How long would she be made to wait for the sensual pleasures promised to her over dinner? Jim opened her door and raised her hand to kiss it. Too long, her inner voice lamented. Car started, windows closed, air conditioning running, they waited for an opening. Jim leaned in to kiss her neck. Honking horns and the revving of idle engines sound-tracked her rising passion: urgent, impatient.

"Jim," she murmured into the ear she was nibbling, "meet me at the back of the car." Anticipation was clear in her words. The confused look on his face was innocent, and sexy. A soft laugh escaped her. "Come on," she coaxed.

Shaylee swung open the rear door and climb in. Jim watched intently as she spread out a quilt. She laid back and reached out for him. His questioning expression melted into a knowing smile. Tinted windows afforded visual privacy. She didn't care who might be listening when her low moans escalated to panting cries.

They checked into the first hotel they found and fell asleep in each other's arms. The Space Needle was outside their window when they woke up in the morning.

By Wednesday afternoon, a heatwave had settled over the Portland-Vancouver area. She could feel the temperature rise higher and higher the further south they drove.

The house was uncomfortable; warm and stuffy. Shaylee called over her shoulder as she changed the climate control setting. "If you want, we can work outside for a while, until the house cools down."

She turned to find Jim in front of her. His eyes were pleading. His smile was shaky with anticipation. Trying to convince them both, she sternly stated, "We really need to get back to work."

He laughed. She laughed. He laughed again.

"Really," she repeated, trying to back away. He scooped her into his arms. Her breath caught in her throat. How easily he carried her. How gently he laid her on the bed. Resistance yielded to passion when he quickly undress himself, but slowly undressed her.

On Friday morning, they woke up at around seven o'clock. The air was as cool as it would be all day, and they decided on an early walk. There were a few shadows the sun hadn't found yet, a few stray breezes the night hadn't let go of.

The ground under a cluster of Douglas Fir trees offered itself up. A cushion of forest debris promised comfort. Dappled sunlight promised cool relief from the rising heat. Jim settled into the spot, stirring a sweet, piney smell. She settled into his lap facing away from him. The fragrance rose stronger, shed fir needles warmed by summer.

Jim leaned forward to kiss the back of her neck. Chills ran a path along Shaylee's spine. Laughter hummed in her throat as he tried to unbutton her blouse. She twisted away and turned to face him. Because she was wearing a light, loose-fitting skirt, it was easy to slip off. Her shirt and panties followed the skirt's path. Clothing tossed away, she pushed Jim to the ground and pulled down his sweat pants, half way. Her fingers traced along the edges of his scars, the story behind them now a part of her.

Satisfied smiles on both their faces, she retrieved her clothes and redressed while he watched. They laid down side by side on the cool ground and looked up through the overhead branches.

"Shaylee," Jim murmured, "who was the greatest love of your life?"

He already knew it wasn't David.

She'd shared a few entertaining stories but had managed to side-step most of his personal questions. Comments like 'We're not talking about me, Jim.' or 'This doesn't have anything to do with the book,' had worked, until now. And his question. In asking who she'd loved the most, he was also asking who'd hurt her the most.

A lingering sigh escaped through lips pursed with concern. "I'm not sure I want to tell you. It will only show how naïve I used to be."

"You know how naïve I used to be," he reminded her.

Used to be. Shaylee felt a smile build up on her face, starting with her lips, moving to her cheek. Yes, used to be.

It was already heating up, but once she'd picked up her notebook and pen, they continued their walk. She mentally steadied herself to tell Jim the most painful story of her life.

"I should have been suspicious by even the way we met, but there I was, so young. Only eighteen. So enthusiastic, so eager to experience whatever came my way; asking everything, questioning nothing. I was on the Admiral's Staff at the Philadelphia Naval Base."

"That's right," he said. "We talked about Philly. You told me you were in the Navy."

"I worked in the Public Affairs Office. My long list of duties included putting messages up on a big marquee inside the front gate. People would request things like, 'Fair Winds And Following Seas Master Chief Houston' for retirement parties. Or 'Welcome Captain and Crew: H.M.S. Starling' when a visiting ship docked. One day I was in the middle of putting up the message, 'Congratulations Mitchell Quinn, Shipyard Employee Of The Month,' when a man pulled up in a shipyard work truck. He was tall, and looked to be around thirty-five. Hazel eyes. Salt-and-pepper hair, an amazing smile on his handsome face. 'Hey, *I'm* Mitchell Quinn.'

"That's how we met. When we started dating, we went out with couples he knew from the base and the shipyard. We spent time with my friends from the Admiral's staff. We went on a sunset cruise, took a trip to Atlantic City. There was a trip to D.C., one to Valley Forge, all kinds of romantic little get-aways.

"He invited me to the wedding of one of his friends. I caught some of the guests giving me sad looks, but had no clue why. The teenage boys were drinking together in a corner of the dance floor, egging each other to ask me to dance. A married man walked up to me and started to flirt. I even caught the bride shooting me a pity look.

"Mitch said he'd never been married. He'd been drafted into the Vietnam War when he was eighteen, only spending a year there, just before the truce. But he said the experience left him so emotionally scarred he was never able to form a lasting relationship with a woman.

"He had a big tan Chevy van with handicapped license plates, explaining that his father had suffered a stroke. The van was used to take him back and forth to doctor appointments. It became clear early on that his mother would need outside help. Mitch started a nursing company to off-set the high costs of in-home care. So, between his shipyard job, taking care of his dad, and running the nursing business, he didn't have a lot of free time.

"When we'd been going out for about four months, he invited me to meet his mother. His father had just died, and she was staying at her daughter Rebecca's house. We drove to a town, I forget the name, about an hour out of Philly. The moment we entered the house, Rebecca rushed a roomful of kids away before I even had time to count them. His brother-in-law stood at the dining room table, glaring at a sandwich he was making. He stared at that half-finished sandwich, rigid, unmoving, the whole time we were there.

"Mitch and his mom sat down in a love seat and started talking. The closest seat was a couch at the other end of a long, narrow room. I sat in that dark room, just sat there, feeling so out of place, and not knowing why. When we started to leave, I passed by the man at the table. 'Nice to meet you,' I said. He looked up from that sandwich, still glaring and visibly shaking, but didn't say anything. I didn't see Rebecca or the kids again.

"It was a weird visit, but it was the first time I'd met any of Mitch's family. And, I think, that was when I shut down my defenses. How could I be suspicious of his motives? I was at his sister's home, meeting his mother. Well, I guess, subconsciously, it was all the proof I needed. I fell, head-over-heels, and landed, hard in love.

"After his father's death, I expected the handicapped license plates to come off Mitch's van. I also thought we'd have more time to spend together. His explanations for both had to do with his nursing company. It was growing quickly and taking up more of his time. He still had the handicapped plates because the van was used for business.

"He had a lot of excuses for breaking promises, changing plans, and canceling our dates. A nursing shift needed to be covered. There were stacks of paperwork to finish. So-and-so needed some medical equipment delivered. His pager went off at all hours."

Jim chuckled. "Pager."

"Yes, pager. It was the early nineties. Sometimes we would be in the middle of a date and he'd have to leave. Sometimes we'd be in the middle of . . . um," Shaylee stopped short. Her next few words were as vague as possible.

"You know, things, and he would pass out from exhaustion."

They returned to the house and, over breakfast, Shaylee finished the story.

"Eventually our time together became less and less, and finally dwindled down to one evening a week. Wednesdays. But I was stupid in love. I didn't care. I was happy with whatever time he was able to carve out of his schedule to spend with me. Even if it was always at my house. Even if we never went to his house. Or spent any more time with his friends or relatives. I don't even remember those excuses."

She was again inside that part of her life, revisiting that love-struck eighteen-year-old; a blissfully happy girl who, because she was in love, felt like a woman for the first time.

"Well, anyway," her voice, her words, pulled her away from the past. "We were together for just under three years. I got out of the Navy and decided to stay there, to be with him. I became a legal secretary. You're from Philly. You know how it is. All the car accidents, all the bus and train accidents, the slip-and-falls. Personal injury lawyers were everywhere. The money was good. The hours were a steady nine-to-five. Five days a week. Weekends and holidays off. I started out working for a small four-man firm."

She laughed when she remembered her first day at 'Cohen, Kaplan, Bluestein and Levitt.'

"I got on the bus that morning, but it was re-routed to take the city streets. The expressway was blocked by a multi-vehicle accident. Almost two hours late, I walked through the door, raised my hands in the air, and tried to speak, but nothing came out. I was so mortified. Alan Levitt's partners were not pleased, but Alan just started to laugh. He said, 'There's no way you would be *this* late on your first day of work if there wasn't a good reason.'

"Alan was a nice man. We became fond of each other very quickly. He would always tease me with, 'You need to find a husband.' After he met Mitch, he told me, 'He's not going to marry you.' But I just shook my head. I didn't believe him. I didn't believe anything but my love.

"It was a nice job, one I didn't want to leave, but I had to. They couldn't offer me any medical benefits or vacation pay, so I built up some experience and then went to work for a bigger firm. Alan was very understanding.

"Well, I was at my new law firm for about six months. Everything was going great. Everything in my life was at a nice, steady, even pace. Then, one day, I struck up a conversation with a woman who had just started working there. She was from the same neighborhood Mitch lived in.

"'Oh, do you know Mitchell Quinn?'

"'No,' she answered, 'but I know of the Quinn family. Did you know one of the brothers is married to a woman in a coma?'

"I answered, 'No. I didn't know that. Which one?'

"'I'm not sure,' was her reply. Her eyes widened before she turned away and went back to her typing.

"And, it happened on a Wednesday. When I got home, Mitch was curled up in my bed, napping. He opened his eyes, saw me, and started to smile.

"The first thing I said to him was, 'Mitch, why didn't you tell me one of your brothers was married to a woman in a coma?'

"He immediately looked away in panic. When he looked back at me, his face was closed and angry.

"After growling, 'I don't want to talk about this,' he bolted out of bed and stomped off to the bathroom.

"I picked up his pager. I looked at the phone number on it, at the number always flashing on that little screen. It was his business number, right? My hands were shaking, but I copied the number down and tucked it away in one of my dresser drawers.

"When he came back to bed, he didn't speak one word about it. I didn't bring it up either. I was in shock. His reaction had confessed everything. I just needed time to let it sink in. A few weeks later, I found enough strength to break things off with him. I remember his distracting accusation of 'You've become so cold lately. I don't understand why.' He stopped talking after I told him he was no longer welcome in my life. I don't remember my exact words. I don't remember much else about that Wednesday night. I do remember hearing my pulse pounding in my ears, crying for hours, and feeling like everything inside of me had broken into pieces.

"And the phone number from his pager? I called it. Someone, I think it was his Mother, answered the phone in an impossibly cheerful voice, 'Quinn residence.' I hung up.

"Well, after that stark ray of reality, I decided it was time to leave the East Coast for good. I was planning out an exit strategy when I found an announcement in my mail from Alan Levitt. He'd started a new firm with two other attorneys. I called to congratulate him. He offered me a job. I told him I was going to move back to Washington. When he asked why, I told him what had happened.

"'Ah,' Alan crooned with much I-told-you-so satisfaction. 'I knew he wouldn't marry you.' I thanked him for his generous job offer. He wished me the best of luck.

"Working through an employment agency was the best way for me to earn money while I packed up my Philadelphia life. I could get in as many hours as I could handle, and leave without having to give notice. As it turned out, I also made more as a temp than as a permanent employee. It was a win-win situation.

"It only took me six months to save up enough. I was on my last assignment, which was a great one. The building was beautiful. The offices were elegant, and the attorneys and staff were great. On my third day there, I had just settled in at my desk when a clerk handed me a stack of files and a transcription tape. I went through five of the files, and picked up the next one on the stack.

"'Leona Quinn and Mitchell Quinn versus...'

"In shock, barely breathing, I read the original lawsuit Mitchell's attorneys had filed with the court. Only a few weeks before their first anniversary, Leona Quinn was taking a cab to meet Mitchell for a romantic dinner. The cab driver cut off a city bus, and the bus couldn't stop in time. It rammed the rear of the cab and pinned it against a building. The cabbie only had minor injuries, but it took two hours for firefighters to free Leona. She flat lined in the ambulance. They were able to revive her heart, but she was admitted to the hospital in a coma. A battery of tests revealed severe brain damage from head trauma and blood loss. A year passed, the coma was deemed permanent. Leona was left in a persistent vegetative state.

"Instead of putting her into a nursing home, Mitchell brought his bride home. With the help of his family, Leona's mother, and hired nurses, he was able to care for her.

"When I finished reading it, I just held that file in my hands. I was numb. I couldn't even feel the paper I was touching. That document told me more about Mitchell Quinn than he ever had. All the details of the case, all the details of his life with a comatose wife. It was so hard to believe. That all the answers to all those questions had been handed to me. Just handed to me.

"The case against the cab company had settled the year before, but Leona had just died. The letter I was given to dictate had to do with her estate.

"I called Mitchell that night. Even after I broke things off with him, he'd always made sure I had a phone number where I could reach him. The number I called was a cell phone. He was driving when he answered, and I told him about the interesting case that had just crossed my desk."

"'What,' he asked, 'about Leni?'

"Hearing him say her name, her nickname. He might as well have sent a bullet through me. He was starting to say something else when I heard a crashing sound in the background."

"'Oh, no,' he said, 'I just got into an accident.'

"I started to laugh, and then, I couldn't stop."

"'It's not funny! It's not funny!' he shouted. 'Fuck you. Fuck you.'

"He was still shouting, I was still laughing, when I hung up."

Shaylee shook her head.

"He conspired with his family and his friends to deceive me. He devastated me. He devastated my life. He later admitted our first meeting was arranged. That he'd asked one of his friends to call in the message for the marquee, then waited until I showed up to change the sign. He eventually confessed to setting up the meeting with his family to lower my suspicions. He knew that once I met them, I would fall in love with him.

"He even confessed to taking advantage of my position on the Admiral's Staff to make social in-roads at work. *And*, he kept trying to justify what he'd done. He kept saying, 'You understand why I couldn't tell you, right? You understand why I couldn't say anything.'"

"I left Philly three weeks after that. The next, and last, time Mitch and I talked, Shawn was around three. The phone company still had a forwarding number on file for me from my old apartment, the one I lived in before I married David. Mitch had changed his phone number and wanted to be sure I had it. He asked if he could come out and visit me. I used some excuse about being too busy.

"A few years later, I bought a new address book. I was transferring the information from the old one to the new one and came across his name and number. I looked at it for a long time. Eventually, I turned that page. When I was done copying the names and numbers I did want to save, I threw the book away."

Lunch finished, Shaylee cleared the table. Jim helped her with the dishes. She'd expected him to ask questions, but he didn't. His silence was a little upsetting at first. When she imagined a few of the questions he might ask, she decided to be relieved instead. Talking about Mitch had brought up a lot of old emotions. Some of them, she wasn't sure she had answers for.

They worked a little later to avoid the heat of the day. The sun finally gave way to a cooling twilight. Shaylee fixed a plate of cold cuts, cheese, and fruit. While she sliced and thinly buttered some French bread, Jim picked out a bottle of wine and two glasses.

The walk to the pool marked a turning point. From day to evening, from work to play. They sat down to face each other across the poolside table, something more tempting than food between them. The meal was fresh and tasty, but it was their thoughts about what was next that fed them.

"Jim," Shaylee started. She didn't want to spoil the mood, or her own anticipation, but had to speak the question that would not leave her mind.

"Was it a mistake to tell you about Mitch?"

He lowered his wine glass to look her in the eyes.

"No," was his simple answer.

Unconvinced, she went on.

"I told you it would make me look naïve. Maybe it was . . ."

Shaylee tensed, at a loss for words.

Sitting straight up in a chair that suddenly felt confining and uncomfortable, she tried again. "Maybe . . ."

"Maybe," Jim offered, "you trusted me enough to share one of *your* deepest, darkest secrets."

At first, she thought he was joking, but he didn't smile. His face wore a thoughtful expression. There was a concerned look in his eyes. It was the same way she looked at him when he told his revealing stories.

"Maybe," she agreed and relaxed back into the chair.

She could have shared a less tragic experience. How would he have known? But she was glad she'd chosen that story, that truth. Even during the telling, there was something different about it. Because, that time, and for the first time, she felt better once it was said. Also, for the first time, that part of her life felt less like an embarrassment and more like an ordeal she'd bravely overcome. Maybe even a rite of passage.

Jim shared his most painful experience with her, and it lead the way to something amazing. Shaylee confessed her most painful story to him, and that part of her past was losing its power over her. Also, something amazing.

Plates empty, wine finished, clothes off, they slipped into the pool. The swaying water pulled heat away from her skin. Her arms and legs cooled. Jim came up behind her, kissed her neck, her ear, along her jawline to her cheek. His hands found their way around her and guided her to the edge of the pool. He climbed out first to lay a soft, thick beach towel over the hard stone floor.

After smoothing it out, he went to her. Hands touching, smiles meeting, laughter mingling, she was out of the water and beside him. Shaylee began to kiss his neck, but he gently eased her away. Jim looked confidently into her eyes as he rested her onto the towel. His kisses began at her neck and moved further down, between her breasts.

"Is this where he hurt you?" Jim asked. "Here?" He moved his lips a fraction of an inch to the left, guessing at where her heart might be. "Here?"

"Yes," she answered, "there."

He kissed that spot again, even more tenderly, and asked in a whisper, "Is that better?"

"Yes," she answered in a whisper. "That's better."

She tried to return his kisses, to match his caresses, but each time he stopped her. He had taken the lead. He had taken control. If sheer tenderness had the power to heal, his lovemaking on that night would have erased every hidden wound and every emotional scar she'd ever had.

# Week Five

Monday was winding down. They were at the end of a chapter, at the end of five o'clock, at the beginning of the evening. He took her hand in his and brushed chiseled lips over the inside of her wrist.

"Shaylee, I was thinking. When I was in school, I took dance classes, but only learned things like the waltz and the foxtrot. So boring. The mosh pits were an anonymous mess, nothing but bump-and-grind. I never got a chance to do anything, you know, romantic."

"That sounds, interesting," was all she could manage.

Thinking gave way to feeling. Warm breath and light kisses moved up her arm, across her shoulder, along her neck.

After breakfast on Tuesday, they picked twenty songs to play on a loop. Some of them were his favorite, some hers. All were mid-tempo; nothing too fast, nothing too slow.

As the music started, Shaylee asked Jim to stand still. Smooth and subtle movements were how she began. Her body danced to him, away from him, only to return again. He reached out to her. She escaped.

The music continued. So did her sensual seduction. Hands lightly touching, hips gently brushing, breasts temptingly near. His body responded. Her need rose and she surrendered to it, dancing into his arms.

Firmly, he grasped her. Gently, he guided her. Together, they found the floor and Jim gave her a different song to dance to.

When that dance was finished, she was the first to speak.

"Our lessons won't get very far at this rate."

Laughing, panting, he managed, "I don't care."

Thursday morning found them dancing, touching, teasing. Music encouraged the mood with its pulsing and throbbing. Shaylee lifted Jim's t-shirt and he stopped moving. Her eager fingers traced over his toned chest.

Down went his sweatpants. He was not fully erect. It was an opportunity, her first opportunity, to explore - to taste - to tantalize - to rouse. His surprised gasps, his drawn-out moans, his firm response, took her from eager to urgent.

"Now, get onto your side," she commanded sweetly. "Perch yourself up on one arm."

He complied.

She turned the music down.

"Don't move," she said as she undressed, not watching, or caring, where her clothes landed. She grabbed a plump pillow from the couch and placed it under his hip. It allowed space between him and the floor, enough room for her to easily slip her leg under him without pinning her down.

She laid down parallel to him and wrapped her legs around him. In that position, Shaylee had more freedom of movement. His weight was not on top of her, and she didn't have to concentrate on balancing above him. She guided him into her, firmly grabbed his buttocks and used the grip to help her balance as their lovemaking began.

"Don't move," she whispered. "Don't move. Let me,"

He complied.

She did move, slow and rhythmic, arching her back to let his chest hair tickle her breasts. They tightened in response. Moaning came to her ears. It was her moaning, but it sounded far off, coming from somewhere else. She was floating, touching nothing, feeling everything. Gasping, forgetting how to breathe, she was overtaken by waves of pleasure. Air found her lungs, filled them and escaped into cries as the waves found their way through her. She collapsed beside Jim, panting.

And then, laughter. His laughter. As she tried to catch her breath, he grabbed her wrists and pushed his body against hers until she was on her back. He lowered his weight fully onto her, pinning her to the floor.

"Don't move," he half-growled, half-sighed, using his knees to spread her thighs apart.

He entered her, began to move inside her.

Slowly, slowly.

His pace remained steady, didn't waiver.

Slowly, slowly.

Beads of sweat broke out onto his forehead.

Slowly, Slowly.

His body froze. He cried out a song of ecstasy. One verse. Two verses. A fading chorus as he quieted and relaxed on top of her. Jim's weight was a satisfying pressure on her still-tingling body. His easing gasps were the ending of his song. She listened to the music. Its simplicity. Its aching beauty.

By Saturday, they'd worked up a loosely orchestrated routine, a sultry, suggestive dance that made them feel as though they were making love with their clothes on. It was that dance that Shaylee took with her into the next week.

# Week Six

Jim's only contact with the outside world was through his agent, Ben Stein-Levine. Any calls from Ben were taken in his room. 'Just got off the phone with my agent,' was the only information he'd ever offered. This Sunday morning was different. The bedroom door opened and Jim's cheerful voice spilled out. "Yeah, Ben, I know. Yes. Yes. Okay. Bye."

He walked briskly by her, set the phone on the table and offered a perfunctory "Good morning, Shaylee'" on his way to the coffee pot.

The question in her eyes was answered with, "Today's the day. Ben gave me the heads up. The phone lines are open."

"Open?" she questioned.

"I didn't want to be distracted while we were working, so I had him handle all my calls. But today's the day. Oh, I just said that. I'm probably going to be getting a lot of calls. A lot."

He took his coffee to the table, sat down in front of his phone, and looked at his watch. With eyes gleaming, he said, "I'm live in five, four, three, two, one."

Shaylee laughed, but, as he'd predicted, the phone rang.

"Hello? Hey, Mom. So good to hear your voice. Yes, I've missed you, too..."

After gently and reluctantly ending the call with his mother, Jim's life started pouring in. Six short calls that sounded like friends and family. Then, a call he cut short with, "Perfect. We'll talk soon."

"Shaylee," Jim barely looked up from his phone, "I just got word from my assistant. He booked me on a red-eye flight for early Sunday morning, so I'll be leaving here at around ten p.m. Saturday night."

Assistant? He'd never mentioned an assistant. She had to guess at the odd travel arrangements. Were they a tactic to help him avoid recognition? The next call came in before he could explain.

That call started out calmly, but became more animated. The one-sided conversation didn't make clear why he was upset, but the pitch of his voice raised as he talked. Things apparently weren't going the way he'd intended. With a terse, "We'll finish this later, okay?" he ended the call.

Shaylee kept busy making breakfast, trying to not overhear him. After all, none of those conversations had anything to do with her.

The phone quieted and she approached him. Her face held a smile and her arms held a tray of breakfast appetizers. He didn't return her smile, or offer to pour some orange juice. He did raise bothered eyes to her and snapped, "I'm not hungry."

Abruptly, he stood and turned away. His retreat was accompanied by the music of his ringtone. The song was loud and strong, but faded as he turned the corner. He closed the door before answering. Soft clattering took up the silence. It came from the tray. Her arms were shaking, upsetting its contents.

She'd never seen Jim so unnerved, and allowed herself the luxury of passing his behavior off as unthinking, not unkind. It was a sliver of rational thought that calmed her shaking.

Shaylee set the tray down and absently walked away from the table. She found herself in front of the kitchen calendar. It showed her the days that had passed, and the number of days ahead. Sunday, September eighth. Their deadline was only six days away. Six days. Six. Days. She looked towards Jim's room. It was the beginning of their last week together and it hadn't started out well. Was this what she had to look forward to?

Over two hours later, Jim approached her, composed and apologetic. As he asked about the previously offered food, his phone sounded off from the bedroom. The game of "How Far Can I Walk Away From My Phone Before It Rings?" continued for three more calls. On his fourth approach, she nodded towards the table. The tray sat where she'd left it. After a quick shoulder shrug and eye roll, he picked up the tray, and was gone again.

Shaylee filled the day with some long neglected chores, first in the house, then, in the yard. It was after five o'clock when she'd finished the sweaty, tiring job of pulling weeds from around the deck. Muscles aching, nerves frayed, she accepted the lounge chair's invitation to sit and rest.

The late summer sun moved towards the western horizon. Its light took on a rich honey color as it met up with the end of the day. When the sun disappeared, the air quickly cooled, prompting Shaylee to go inside. She poured a glass of milk and fixed a sandwich, her movements the only noises in the room. Three plates of leftovers set out, she picked up her dinner and headed towards the stairs. A stop in front of the hallway leading to Jim's room. Door closed. No sound. No movement. She went to her own room to eat her first meal in weeks alone.

On Monday morning, apprehension escorted Shaylee up to the kitchen. She found an impressive mess of half empty plates and dirty dishes. The ringing doorbell brought Jim rushing out of his room and past her. It was a courier delivering a package. He signed for it, thanked the man, closed the door and headed back the way he'd come.

"A proposed movie script," he answered her curious gaze. As he passed by, his gait caused a breeze behind him. It was cold, and held the scent of his cologne.

He appeared again, for breakfast, empty-handed. The package and his phone were out of sight, but they were obviously still on his mind. His preoccupation took its own spot at the table with them. Several times, she had to pull his mind back from the thoughts that kept stealing his attention. On that day she was able to get him to focus on their work, but, she couldn't pull his thoughts back to her. They stopped talking about the book and he stopped talking.

During dinner, she tried to chase away her own uneasiness with lighthearted chatter. Picking the endless subject of Northwest weather, Shaylee began a nervous monologue. His face reacted to her conversation, but there was a blankness in his eyes. He'd pasted a fake smile on his lips, and there was a noticeable absence of his voice responding to hers.

The pace of his fork moving back and forth quickened. When the food was gone, he stood up. With a nod and the sparse explanation of, "I've got a script to read through," he walked away. She watched his retreat, relieved he didn't look back. If he had, he would have seen the hurt expression she knew she wore.

Again, Shaylee went to her own room to sleep that night, becoming aware of an old silence that was edging its way back in. It was patiently waiting to replace Jim's presence with its own.

Tuesday morning, Jim found her quiet and reserved. She moved around the kitchen slowly, keenly feeling her own weight as she walked. He came to the table without his script or phone. She approached him with a plate of hash browns and fried ham. He was studying her face. She set the plate down in front of him and met that gaze with a weak smile. He visibly relaxed.

"I am so, so sorry about yesterday, Shaylee, a-a-and, the day before. See," he held up open, empty hands and gave her a flirty smile. "No phone. No script."

Those hands reached out to her, but she backed away. A startled look flashed across his face.

Gently, she scolded, "Jim, you know we need to get right to work. We're almost done."

"You're right," he agreed, his surprise overcome by confusion. "Yes, you're right."

Shaylee watched his reaction numbly. Only a few days before, that scene would have played out in a very different way. Her disappointment rose slowly, but it did arrive, dull and aching. Without even thinking, she'd physically withdrawn from his reach, from his touch, from him. Her first retreating steps. What her body had instinctively reacted to, her mind was beginning to understand.

Following Shaylee's lead, Jim focused on work. They stopped only for a quick and preoccupied lunch. At four forty-two p.m., after an intense and lengthy read-through, they agreed. Their work together on the book was done. A sad type of relief came first, but was replaced with growing excitement. During their call to the publisher, they scheduled a video conference for the following morning. Nine o'clock Wednesday morning.

It had been raining, but stopped while she washed the breakfast and lunch dishes. A walk out onto the deck led to a discovery: new growth. Thin streaks of bright green grass spiked up through crumpled mats of pale, brittle stalks - pieces of summer the sun hadn't baked away. The seeds of dead and dying plants also began to sprout. She'd always thought of it as a 'Second Spring.' Made up of differently shaped and textured seedlings, miniature forests covered the ground. Some were in large patches or island-like oases. The little landscapes were so beautiful she tried to avoid stepping on them. They were all bright miracles of green that would begin to melt into the soil with the first frost.

A smiling Jim appeared in the doorway, and stopped, framing himself inside it. He was half in, half out of the door. He was half in, half out of her life. Shaylee couldn't return his smile. Too many thoughts weighed down the corners of her mouth. After he asked, "You feeling up to a walk?" they felt a little less heavy. He was trying to soothe her with a vestige of their summer routine, and she was willing to be soothed.

Their slow pace and small talk were touched by thick mist. The mist graduated to a sprinkle. The sprinkle turned to rain. The rain became a downpour. Shaylee suggested, "The barn," and ran towards it. Jim passed her and ran ahead, disappearing around a curve in the trail. When she rounded the curve, the barn came into view. Jim had finished rolling open one of the large, heavy doors and was waiting for her.

She ran through the opening and past him because she couldn't stop. He reached out for her, but missed. She was panting but still heard the door close. Jim came to her. They took turns laughing and kissing. He wiped a drop of rain off her nose. She wiped a few off his forehead. Their arms filled with each other. They stayed that way for a long time - her head resting against his chest, his chin resting on top of her head. The feel of his body. The heat of his skin. She didn't want to let go. Jim wouldn't let go. Only when she began to pull away did he.

After scanning the room, he moved towards a stack of straw bales. Jim sat down on the floor in front of one, leaned back against it, and made a space between his legs for her. Shaylee took the place he offered and his arms wrapped around her. She snuggled against him and shivered.

"It's starting to feel like autumn," she said.

"Mmmmm," Jim hummed a sound of pleasure in her ear. He pressed forward and started to gently rub against her, "it's starting to feel like Shaylee, too."

He was kissing her neck and unbuttoning her shirt. She was laughing, feeling his hands work their way further, and further, down. The barn disappeared. The last two days disappeared. The cold disappeared. She found herself on top of him, his body heat rising to warm her. He found his way inside her, another kind of heat to warm them both.

He moaned in release. She stopped moving, and couldn't help but smile at his expression of pure pleasure. Then, another look crossed his face. It was barely concealed. It was brief, but clear, and, unmistakable. Contempt. Impatient contempt.

She could almost hear what he was thinking. She could almost feel his eyes rolling. Her mouth fell open. Her breath stuck in her throat.

With his eyes closed, he might have been unaware she was looking at him. Maybe he thought the expression would go unnoticed, or, maybe, he'd meant for it to be noticed. He was a consummate actor. She couldn't imagine it being an accidental slip. Had he planned it, purposely done it? Was this his way of putting an exclamation point at the end of their time together? The past few days had been one thing; Jim's priorities and obligations reclaiming their place in the forefront. But this?

Too soon. It was all happening too soon. They still had days left, didn't they? They still had time left. Didn't they?

Shaylee tried to inhale. Couldn't. Swallowed. Tried again. Coughed softly. When she could breathe in, she took a deep breath and arched her back in a simulated stretch. Jim sat up and kissed between her breasts. It was an intimate, tender gesture. Wanting to pull away, but not being able to, she could only beg silently, *'No, please, no.'*

Her eyes snapped closed against the pressure building behind them. She tried to will the tears away, but shock was giving way to emotions. They began their own storm inside her, and had a mind of their own.

Careful to face away, Shaylee stood up and retrieved her clothes. She shook off some of the loose straw before putting them on. Next, she found her notepad and pen, relieved they were a little damp but still usable. Turning her back to him, she started filling the blank page with random words and scribbles. Without turning around, she suggested, "Jim, why don't you head back. I just got an idea. I need a few minutes, okay?" Known to duck away to document bursts of inspiration, Jim shouldn't think twice about the request.

Laughing, he said, almost to himself, "Already starting on your next novel."

She nodded, but didn't speak. Behind her were the sounds of him shaking off his clothes, getting dressed, and then, footsteps. He re-opened the door and started to walk away. She heard him stop and turn around.

Tears slid down her face.

Footsteps again, going back up the trail, in the direction of the house.

Tears fell onto the paper. One of the things she'd learned in her marriage to David was how to quietly cry.

Shaylee slipped into her bedroom unnoticed. To the bathroom, to the vanity. Planning to re-apply make-up, she looked into the mirror. Her reflection didn't show streaked foundation or running mascara. It showed a woman who just had the ending of one of her own stories written for her.

A soft ache filled her chest, moving in and out as she breathed. A tremor started at her core. It built. It spread. It became stronger, like something physical was trapped inside, trying to escape. In one overwhelming wave, she felt herself begin to grieve, and knew there was nothing she could do to stop it.

She lowered her head and cupped her face in her hands. A new sadness, feelings of loss for Jim, pulled the breath from her throat and the tears from her eyes.


He was calling her name, his voice questioning and concerned, from the bedroom doorway. She walked out of her bathroom, towards him. She'd had enough time to wipe away tear stains. The pain on her face was a mask she did not have the power to remove. When she was close enough to see his eyes, and the guilt in them, she stopped. She was also close enough to see an unspoken apology dance across his face.

A stray tear fell down her cheek. Jim wasn't close enough to wipe it away, but he saw it, and started to raise his arm, to reach out to her. Stopping himself, his hand gripped into a loose fist. His thumb brushed over the tops of his clenched fingers and the arm dropped to his side. He stretched his hand out and relaxed it. His arm relaxed. His shoulders slumped. His head bowed. She felt heavy, too heavy to move. All she could do was watch Jim as complete helplessness deflated him from the inside out.

Words were . . . unnecessary.

He raised his head, squared his shoulders, and turned around.

Her eyes relaxed. Jim became a blur, but everything else around her came into soft focus. Was this some kind of shock? She couldn't make herself look away, but could close her eyes, and did. Mercifully, she didn't have to witness what happened next – Jim walking away from her.

Shaylee numbly made her way upstairs, to the kitchen, and started dinner. How could it happen? The events, all the amazing events of the past two months, erased. Just erased. Replaced with a hollow emptiness that would very soon evolve into something else. Something fierce and painful. Why was she even standing there, preparing a meal as though everything was fine? Rinsed romaine lettuce leaves in the sink, cheddar cheese biscuits on the counter, and she didn't remember putting them there. Leaving everything where it was, she ambled away. Back down the stairs. Back to her room. A long, hot bath. Loud music. Soft crying. She went through the motions of preparing for sleep, already knowing that sleep wouldn't come.

After settling into bed, she pulled a new notebook from the top of a stack she kept in her bedside table drawer. Her eyes rested on a piece of fresh, clean paper. How long did she stare at that blank page before it came alive with visions of Jim?

Shaylee looked up, away, down, around, but the room's darkness was a blank screen for her visions to play on. The past weeks ran like a highlights reel, over, and over, and over. His voice. His stories. His secrets. All the times he whispered or laughed her name. What her lips taught him. What his smiles taught her. Moans and sighs and . . .

She thought she was done crying, but her pain found more tears. Some of them she wiped away. Some of them disappeared into the blankets. Some landed on the paper. Eventually, when they stopped, she was able to concentrate. When she was able to concentrate, a question started running through her mind. It was one she knew she wouldn't be able to bring herself to ask Jim, a question she wrote down:

## What did it mean to you?

¤ ¤ ¤ ¤ ¤ ¤ ¤ ¤ ¤ ¤ ¤ ¤ ¤

On Wednesday morning, Shaylee's radio alarm came on in the middle of a weather report. It sounded like the announcer was speaking in a foreign language.

The first words her mind could focus on were, "and the time is seven-oh-four."

As she found her way through a veil of sedated emotions, she started to remember. As she started to remember, her heart began to pound. As her heart pounded, the layers of sleep broke away. Consciousness came, weak at first, but stronger, and more unrelenting. It pushed her closer to reality, closer to what lay ahead of her: her last day, her last morning, her last hours, with Jim.

How long had she slept? It couldn't have been more than a few hours. Her last look at the clock was at three a.m. and she'd still been wide awake. The notebook. Where was the notebook? She felt around in the bed, and when she found it, it went back to its spot, at the top of the stack, inside the drawer.

For the first time since Jim had come to stay with her, she used the downstairs kitchen to make her morning tea. With an hour and a half until the conference call, she took her time getting ready. At eight fifty-five, she went directly to the computer. Jim was already in the office, sitting in front of a fire he'd started, holding a cup of steaming coffee.

'So,' she thought, 'he does know how to work a coffee maker.'

They were in the same room, but not together. Separately, they waited for the call from Tern Publishing. The only sounds between them came from the fire.

A tone from the computer signaled the beginning of the conference call. When the call ended, Shaylee rushed to the kitchen, relieved to have the routine of making breakfast ahead of her. The remnants of last night's attempt at dinner were still there, waiting for her. Beyond saving, the wilted lettuce was thrown out, but she set the biscuits on a plate and put them in the microwave. They would taste good with a sautéed mushroom omelet.

Without thinking, she called out, "Jim, you hungry?"

Hesitant steps brought him into the room. "Ummm, y-y-e-es-s-s."

Jim alternated his attention from the food on his plate to the manuscript in his hand. She asked him about it, and listened for any hint of emotion in his voice. What she heard was detached politeness. From across the table, she looked for any sign of recognition in his steel-blue eyes. What she saw in them was distance.

In her sleep-deprived state, concentrating wasn't easy. She didn't have a lot of control over where her mind wandered. At any moment, Shaylee expected him to look up, smile, and tell her how pretty she was. Or stand up and come around the table to give her a lingering kiss. Neither of those things happened.

Remembering something funny Jim had said a few weeks ago, she laughed softly. Without thinking, she reached out to take his hand, but stopped. He noticed the gesture, and then, pretended not to.

Eyes held fast to his manuscript, he didn't move when Shaylee collected the dishes. A controlled, monotone voice interrupted the sounds of her washing them.

"I'll be catching a flight out today."

Shock stilled her hands long enough to hear the silence around them. Quickly, noisily, desperately, the splashing and clanging started again, so she wouldn't have to hear what came next. The sound of Jim leaving the room.

He was gone for thirty, forty, forty-five minutes. She felt every moment pass, but even that time went by impossibly fast.

Straight backed and stone-faced, he marched past her, a suitcase in each hand. (Left profile going out.) Her grip tightened around a teacup she didn't even realize she was holding. She set it down on the counter, and waited, until he walked past her again. (Right profile coming in.) Through dry, blinking eyes, she watched him conduct his leaving parade. (Second trip, arms full.) She saw a man preparing to walk out of her life, and the only thing she knew about that man - he wasn't Jim.

The man in front of her was closed off. He wasn't the thoughtful companion she'd spent the third week of July with. The man carrying every physical trace of himself out of her house was rigid and cold. He wasn't the open and honest storyteller she'd come to know. That man wasn't the injured innocent who'd trusted her with his secret. He wasn't the tender lover she'd touched, and, shown how to touch. (Third trip, suitcase in one hand, keys in the other.) That man, the one she'd spent the past six weeks with, he was gone. He wasn't Jim anymore. He was James Vincent, and he was a stranger.

The stranger approached her. His hands gripped around her upper arms, holding her firmly in place and at arm's length. Afraid of what she might, or might not see, she closed her eyes when the stranger gave her a chaste kiss.

Shaylee was hurt, but couldn't find any anger. There hadn't been time to teach Jim good-bye.

Afraid of what he might see in her eyes, she kept them closed. Not a good idea. Temporary blindness only amplified the sounds of him leaving her house. Opening them, she saw the kitchen door ajar and walked towards it, but the porch door was open too. She tried not to look through it, but couldn't stop herself. Jim was opening his car door.

He came into sharp focus, and his surroundings became a soft blur. She heard her own footsteps, her own breathing, as she walked across the porch, towards him. The recycled glass wind chime told her a breeze had pushed in through the open doorway. The song caught Jim's attention. He turned, saw her, froze. She walked to the edge of the porch, and stopped.

Their eyes met, the twenty-odd feet between them its own good-bye. He straightened up and took a deep breath. She straightened up and took a deep breath. He smiled an innocent smile and waved. She returned his smile and waved. Her arm dropped, but she held the smile on her face as he got into the car. The smile held as tires crunched over her gravel driveway. When he looked into the rear-view mirror, one last time, she was smiling. When the car disappeared down the hill, so did the smile.

She closed and locked the doors behind her, wishing she could lock out her emotions as easily as she could the cold. Trying not to think about him didn't work. One thought pushed away just made room for others. The distractions she invented kept her busy, but didn't keep her from crying. So, Shaylee looked at the rest of that day through the tears in her eyes.

# The Next Chapter

From the moment she walked through Jim's door until the moment he walked out of hers, she'd tried to appreciate every one of those days, those hours, those minutes. But the more she'd wished time would slow down, the faster it went. Then he left. And when he left, he took time with him.

Full days became empty. Excited voices fell silent. She looked around to find herself alone. The sudden transition sent her mind to extreme places. From peace to panic. From euphoria to fear. From stark and vivid remembering to wondering if he'd ever been there at all.

When time found her again, it was Sunday morning. She was wandering around the house, lost in familiar surroundings. Every window she passed, she looked out of. They all showed her an unsettled sky. First black clouds. Then rain. Then white clouds. Then sun. The weather echoed Shaylee's own moods. First calm, then storm, then into and out of the unmeasured places between.

Trying to gauge her feelings wasn't easy. They kept changing, like the answer when she asked herself, 'Am I ready to face the book again?'

She sat down in front of the computer. The soft sound of rain on the window panes was a little bit of mood music. A few things to get out of the way first. Bring up e-mails. Answer e-mails. Erase e-mails. She'd allowed herself four whole days for self-pity wallowing. Wasn't that enough? The rain stopped. Next, check the business line for voice mail messages. Listen to voice mail messages. Erase voice-mail messages. Okay. Now. Bring up document title. Stare at document title. Sip tea. Cold tea. Tea in need of re-heating.

On her way back to the office with her steaming cup, she passed the laundry room. Sheets. She wanted to put freshly laundered sheets on her bed. It only took a few minutes to load and start the washer. Check outside. The sun was blinking in and out of white clouds with dark gray bellies. Back to the computer. Back to the selected file. Back to working up her courage.

Click . . . open. She'd been holding her breath. Out came a weak gasp of relief. There. That wasn't so bad. The title page glowed on the screen. Her heart was still in place. Not in her throat. Not pulsing in her ears. Good. Feelings. Feelings? What was she feeling? Wait. Wait for it.

She smiled. There it was: like a favorite possession she'd been forced to share had been given back to her. It was hers again. All hers. Maybe not for long, but at least for a little while. She could ignore the pressure, forget the deadlines, and hold the world at bay. It was time to experience "Holding Tinsel In My Hands" in complete privacy. No distractions. No interruptions. Just her and the stories, all of the beautiful stories.

She pored over it, made her own changes, added her own ideas and insights. Heightened emotions could have worked against her, but the passionate energy she'd been left alone with found its way into her writing.

There were a few emotional pitfalls. Well, there were a lot of emotional pitfalls, but there was also a new feel to the passing of time. Minutes progressed by ideas. Hours moved along through concepts. Morning slipped away. The afternoon disappeared. When she thought to look out the windows, sunlight had turned into shadows. She let out a deep, satisfied breath. It felt good to again be surprised by the end of the day.

Soon after her windows darkened, the words on the screen began to blur, so she turned the computer off. When the computer went off, the memories switched on. Then came Jim. Then came the ghosts to fill the quiet, empty spaces. They stayed the night. They were there first thing every morning.

So went the third week of September.

¤ ¤ ¤ ¤ ¤ ¤ ¤ ¤ ¤ ¤ ¤ ¤ ¤ ¤

After dinner, Shaylee went through Monday's mail. In it was a letter, and a document, from Jim's Lawyer:

**Dear Ms. Simon:**

**Per James Vincent's wishes, please find the enclosed document. In it, Mr. Vincent authorizes and gives you full creative control over his autobiography, "Holding Tinsel In My Hands".**

She skimmed through the rest of the letter in disbelief. It ended:

**If you have any questions, please contact my office.**

**Sincerely,**

She re-read the letter, then started to read the document. Everything looked right.

In compliance with the agreement between James Vincent, Shaylee Simon, and the aforementioned publishing corporation...

She folded back the first page. Near the bottom of the second page was Jim's signature. Below that, a yellow sticky note:

```
Shaylee -
This book goes
nowhere without
your written
consent - J.
```

First came a shockwave. Once it had run its way over her, she couldn't help but feel anger. Jim's gesture seemed a little cruel, almost like some type of punishment. She went out onto the deck. Several deep breaths. Pause. Several more. They were supposed to be relaxing, but made her dizzy. Maybe a walk would calm her down.

Her stride fluctuated somewhere between a march and a hike. She didn't realize she was taking her anger out on herself until her feet started to hurt and she was gasping for breath. Panting, she stopped, looking up into the trees. Some of the deep green maple leaves were already turning gold. The sun's light was fading, but it wasn't even seven o'clock. Both were signs of summer's loosening hold.

She thought back to her first meeting with Jim. During that meeting, she'd made promises. Promises of quality and accuracy. Promises he remembered, and was counting on her to keep.

A raindrop fell on her cheek as she made a slow, gentle return to the house. There was no way she could concentrate on writing, so she let her mind go to auto-pilot. Dishes rinsed. Dishwasher loaded. Kitchen counters wiped down. Computer off. Downstairs. Fill bathtub. Soak in bathtub.

Anger gave way to questioning. It was a generous show of faith on Jim's part, right? Shouldn't she feel proud, flattered?

Reruns on the television. Still raining. Or had it stopped and started again? She wasn't sure. A groggy walk to bed. Dreamless sleep.

Morning. Tuesday morning. Tuesday morning amnesia that melted slowly. A rush of warmth to her face. Jim. Jim's document. Jim's trust. One eye open. Sunlight. Both eyes open. Sunshine. Breakfast. Read eight days' worth of newspapers to avoid checking for messages. Check for messages. Voice mail? No. E-mail? Nothing. Relief.

One of the things she was afraid of, a fear she shared with Jim, was what might happen to the manuscript once it was out of their hands. During contract negotiations, she'd waived her own creative rights, wanting to be seen as a team player. There weren't any regrets, at first. But, as the stories took shape and the chapters were set into place, Shaylee's time and attention began to feel like an investment. Her name was on the book, too. It was in smaller print (much smaller print), but it was there. And in it were some of her own experiences, hidden among the words and between the lines of James Vincent's life story.

Lunch. Another walk, with her camera. The berry vines and low shrubby trees had started their transition. Red, orange, and brown leaves were even prettier with a backdrop of blue sky and a layer of dappled shadows.

Through the camera's telephoto lens, Shaylee searched for hidden details in the changing forest. Her efforts were rewarded with two lovely scenes: a tiny metallic green bee on a daisy and Rose of Sharon petals highlighted with summer sun and touched with mauve shadows.

The distraction did not stop the wrestling match going on in her mind. She should feel grateful for the second chance, shouldn't she? It was an opportunity she'd mistakenly given up, and it had been graciously returned to her.

Back to the house, the warm, dry house. Check for messages again. Still nothing? Strange. An attempt to get back to the writing. Forty minutes of blinking at the same paragraph.

The document again found its way into her hands. Her finger found Jim's note and traced the edges of the square little piece of paper. She looked at his handwriting, read the note again. Then, finally, came understanding. His decision, his actions, they were a sign of his confidence in her, but there was also a subtle message. Jim had listened to her. He had remembered. He had . . . responded.

When she walked into her office on Wednesday morning, the first thing she did was check for messages. Still nothing. Why? She looked at the attorney's letter again. Copies were sent to everyone involved, but no one had called her?

At ten a.m. a call did come in, from her lawyer. "Well, well, well, Miss Shaylee." Joseph McConaughey's voice held a tantalizing undertone. He was tasting his own words and enjoying the flavor. She could hear the impish grin in his voice. "It looks like our Mr. Vincent was quite impressed with you."

The next call came in twenty minutes later, a man introducing himself as John Lambert. He explained that he was the Senior Vice President of Tern Publishing Company and had been put in charge of her project. He sounded like Nixon addressing a press conference.

"I have concerns, Ms. Simon. Shaylee. Many concerns."

Mr. Lambert was true to his word. She listened to several minutes of his 'concerns.' Did she have any idea what she was getting into? Did she know how important the project was? Did she understand that certain standards had to be met? Did she feel qualified for the task?

He ended his monologue with, "The integrity of this company is at stake, and if I feel this project is being compromised in any way. . . " His silence finished the sentence.

"Mr. Lambert. John." She jumped in quickly, just let him know she wasn't intimidated, then paused. It was time she needed to carefully pick her next words. "I had no idea Jim was going to do this. I mean, I'm still in shock. But, it's what he wants. I respect that, and I hope," a pause, for effect, "you do too."

He snapped, "Well, yes, I do. Of course I do." There was furious typing in the background. "I'm sending you our publishing practices and standards manual. It spells out all of our rules and guidelines. Please consult them before you submit your finished draft."

A thought struck her. "John, when did you get your copy of the letter?"

"It came in this morning's mail. Why?"

A more pointed question. "What's the postmark on the envelope?"

Rustling noises. "Yesterday. It's postmarked yesterday."

She didn't answer. She couldn't. Jim had given her two days alone with the news. Two full days. Time he'd guessed she would need. Realization constricted her throat. She shook her head and tried to swallow, but couldn't. He'd done it again, touched her in a way that reached every part of her.

Shaylee managed a hoarse whisper. "Oh, look." It took a few hard swallows to find her voice again. "Here it is. Here's your e-mail. It just came in. I'm going to get started on this right now. Lots of work to do. Bye."

She ended the call before he could say anything more, so that nothing could interrupt the coming feelings. A small celebration of Jim's awareness. Some proof of his consideration. She felt a little less foolish, a little less taken advantage of, a little less sad. She would never be able to accuse him of not caring. Not ever. Tears came, tears she did not try to stop. They fell slow and steady, down upturned cheeks, over a delicate smile.

The business line's calls were allowed to go to voice mail. The cell phone was rendered silent. The manual and accompanying documents totaled two hundred and sixty-eight pages. It took most of the day to read through. As she read, she took notes. When she was done, there were thirty pages of handwritten notes to type up. By the time that was finished, it was long past sunset, almost ten p.m. A deep, lingering sigh escaped as she shook her head. The first battle was fought and won, but it was just the beginning of the war.

¤ ¤ ¤ ¤ ¤ ¤ ¤ ¤ ¤ ¤ ¤ ¤ ¤ ¤

Each chapter was read and re-read. It was compared to the manual's guidelines, a time-consuming and mind-numbing task. Her condensed notes made the job a little easier, but not much. When the comparison work was done, she submitted her finished draft. It was Monday morning, the last day of September. Jim had been gone for two weeks and five days.

The least she'd hoped for was enough time to take one long, slow, beautiful autumn drive. Tern Publishing's staff had other plans. The first recommendations came in before four o'clock. Her hands flew up and one single exclamation flew out as a frustrated squeal. "Really?"

By Thursday, she didn't even recognize her own life: glued to the computer from eight a.m. to eight p.m., being tag-teamed by seven different people. Seven different personalities. Seven different sets of ideas. Infighting and disagreements filled the places in her head where creativity needed to be. And the outline; the torturous, fact-filled outline? It pushed its way from a fading nightmare back into the forefront. Because of the detailed notes she'd taken during her interviews with Jim, she had to work with the fact-checker and go, over, everything - again!

The editors wanted to make cuts she thought were important. They wanted to change things she knew were relevant. It was also no surprise that John Lambert's opinions contradicted everyone else's. The higher-ups let her know they were being called in too often to settle disputes. There were times she was tempted to give in, but at those times, she looked at Jim's sticky note, and was able to fight the urge.

A call came in from Editor-In-Chief, Harold Mayhew-Reese. He was attempting to launch a pre-emptive strike on the next chapter up, Jim's accident chapter. She hadn't met him, but pictured an overweight man sporting a puffy face and an outdated suit. His attitude was bothered and arrogant.

"Shaylee, I think I know what's coming next. I think you're going to want to leave this chapter uncut." Abruptly his tone changed, to that of a father scolding his misbehaving child. "We both know it's too long, don't we?" He paused, a condescending gesture, to make sure she understood what he was saying. "We both know it goes into way too much detail, doesn't it? Now look, how about we . . ."

Harold's voice disappeared into a flashback. Jim, telling her the story for the first time. Those first reactions, she felt them again. Her own whispers of comfort, they were in her ears again. The thick words and hushed phrases that had passed between them as they wrote. They were all things she could never, would never, forget.

And the night Jim read the finished chapter? Her chest ached when that scene replayed in her head. The expressions on his face. His appreciation. His gratitude. His loss of words, and her attempt to help him find some. Everything that happened wasn't just remembered, it was re-experienced.

When she focused back in on Editor-In-Chief, Harold Mayhew-Reese, he was reading from the chapter. His sarcastic, mocking voice drilled straight through her skull into her brain.

It took all of her self-control to not scream the words, "Stop it, Harry. Stop it. Right now." It took almost as much to continue without crying. "You weren't there. You have no idea what you're talking about. You didn't see the look on Jim's face when he read that chapter, the full chapter, but I did, and . . . and, *(Jim's face. She closed her eyes and she could see Jim's face.)* you can believe me when I tell you, he wouldn't want anything changed."

"Now see here Shaylee, you can't . . ."

"Not one thing, Harry. You will change (a deep breath to steady her voice) not, one, thing."

Harold's answer was, wisely, silence.

She waited a polite amount of time before ending the call with a sweetly voiced, "Thanks for calling Harry. It's always good to hear from you."

Without thinking, she got up from the computer and walked to her wall of windows. Immediately, she regretted it. Outside was an autumn day that would go by too fast, and, without her in it. She could only watch, from behind glass, the sun cross the sky a little lower every day. She could only notice, from inside, that the lower the sun's path was, the more shadows there were to find. The patterns that fell across her pool house were different from summer's patterns. They were a new set of messages written by a changing season.

A break here and there to watch the changing colors. Some stolen time on the deck to smell the dying leaves. To touch and be touched by the October air. They were all tantalizing previews that teased her senses and left her wanting more.

Tern Publishing was closed on Sundays. It was her only chance to get out of the house. Unfortunately, she had to pack a week's worth of shopping and errands into that one day.

On one of those mad-dash Sundays, Shaylee was driving home, exhausted from a seven-hour trip. The plan was to pull into the driveway before sundown, but a flash of movement caught her eye. Starlings, in a murmuration at least a thousand strong, were flying in a synchronized cloud over a neighbor's pasture. She found a place to pull over and got out. Close enough to hear the hushed sounds of fluttering wings, she was still far enough away to see the shapes the flock made against the sky. It was a moving abstract. Complex swirls, jagged circles, misshapen blocks; no recognizable pictures, but still, art. In one sudden dive, they poured out of the sky and spread out, landing within inches of each other over the ground.

A mass of little heads bobbed, disappearing below and popping up above, the dying grass. The birds called and sang. They squabbled and screeched. No one song or separate voice could be heard over the others. The sound of all those starlings together was a special kind of confusion, a miracle of noise. She stood, unmoving. The sun inched its way below the horizon and the birds were lost in the darkening field.

A sudden silence was followed by rushing wings. The flock was airborne again, flying towards the setting sun. Maybe those birds were trying to outrun the shadows, or even the night itself.

¤ ¤ ¤ ¤ ¤ ¤ ¤ ¤ ¤ ¤ ¤ ¤ ¤ ¤

It was the second Wednesday of October. Jim had been gone twenty-eight days, and she'd been thinking about him almost non-stop. Would that change when her work on the book was done? She'd made it to her final obligation, one last conference call, one last read-through. The next stage, design, included the artwork, typography, and cover. They were all choices made by Jim during their last conference call.

That call. That morning. She took a shaky breath and closed her eyes. Emotions tried to find her, but she pushed them away. Not yet. It wasn't time yet. Her day was full, every hour, every minute of it scheduled. After dinner would be better. Much better. After dinner, she could turn on some soft music, settle into a warm bath, and surrender to the memories.

On October Nineteenth, the final changes were agreed to. The publishing date was confirmed: November Fifteenth. "Holding Tinsel In My

Hands" would be released on-line and in paperback a full week before Black Friday.

Shaylee didn't count the days on the calendar Jim had been gone. She counted the days left in October: twelve. It wasn't as much time as she'd hoped for, but there was enough of Autumn left to enjoy. The weather had stayed calm, and, because there hadn't been any major storms, much of the foliage was still intact.

Many of the leaves held onto their branches. Leaves that cast lively shadows and made quiet sounds in the wind. Leaves that fell in random paths to the ground when they did let go, and sounded like fairy footsteps when they landed.

It was Saturday, November Second. The storm she'd been dreading was forecast on the evening news. Late Sunday afternoon, the system that had built up over the Pacific Ocean worked its way inland. Dark clouds climbed over the horizon, filling the sky. The winds didn't pick up until after the sun set. At least she wouldn't have to watch the last autumn leaves being torn from their trees.

Settling into bed, she heard the wind's voice change many times. Leaves and twigs hitting against the windows made scraping noises and tiny crashes. Deeper into the blankets, closer to sleep, she let go of the day. The tempest's surreal song flickered in and out with her fading consciousness.

When she woke up, it was as quiet outside as it was inside. The first thing she thought about was Jim. The second thing she thought about was the storm. After breakfast, she put on an oversized sweater and thick jeans. Next came a coat, scarf, gloves. Stepping out onto a deck decorated with autumn debris, she tested the air. Was it cold enough for a hat? No. Her ears should be safe.

Not long into her walk, she remembered something she did love about late autumn. The stark, impressive structures of naked trees. With the leaves gone she could see the colors, the ridges, the patterns of the trunks. Thick main branches reached out of the trunks like moss-covered arms. Smaller, more intricate branches grew, like hands and fingers, from those. They spread up and they opened out. They tangled into each other and into the surrounding trees. Overhead, the confused branches twisted into puzzles of coarse lace; new outlines that would create different shadows for winter. On the ground, fallen leaves were laid out like designer carpeting at her feet.

She walked past the grove of young Douglas Firs, one of the places she'd made love with Jim. There it was, the twinge. Then, a spark in her brain, the warning that she was going to start thinking about him again. He'd been gone for over two months, close to the same amount of time they'd spent together.

All around her property was wreckage from the storm: fallen limbs, broken branches, damaged trees. Inside her was personal damage from the storm of Jim. The trees would heal by spring. Would she?

Her mind wouldn't stop telling her stories. Some were the stories Jim had told her. Some were the stories she'd told him. There were the ones they'd written together, and the ones they'd made together. They were vivid, honest memories that didn't waiver or change. Again and again they played out, in the light, in the dark, asleep, awake, and she didn't even try to stop them.

Thinking about Jim was painful, but not thinking about him was torture. She might still be reeling from the hurt and loss, but there was one thing she wasn't doing: standing on the sidelines of her own life, looking in and wondering 'What if?' Those damn what ifs. They could have taken up just as much room in her thoughts. They could have stolen the same amount of time from her. But they could never be as interesting as the memories he'd given her.

When Jim came into her life, he reminded her how all-consuming and intoxicating a romantic journey could be. His leaving reminded her of how long it could take to wrap her heart around good-bye. Her feelings might be confusing, and maybe a little scary, but what she was going through, even the worst of it, reminded her what the heart was meant for.

¤ ¤ ¤ ¤ ¤ ¤ ¤ ¤ ¤ ¤ ¤ ¤ ¤ ¤

On November Fifteenth, Tern Publishing Company ceremoniously released "Holding Tinsel In My Hands." The first reviews were generous, more than she'd hoped for:

*"Intimate. Insightful."*

*"A well-told, honest story."*

*"It's no surprise that Shaylee Simon has produced another quality work."*

¤ ¤ ¤ ¤ ¤ ¤ ¤ ¤ ¤ ¤ ¤ ¤ ¤

It was the last day of November, and Shaylee woke up to a foggy landscape. The sun was still in hiding, so she couldn't tell if the sky was cloudy or clear. A few minutes into her morning routine, she was in the upstairs kitchen and the fog had thickened.

From her office window, she watched it turn from grayish-white to gold. With the computer booting up, she returned to her steeped tea, adding sugar and cream. The sun couldn't shine through the thick haze, but, somehow, sunrise colors found their way into the fog. Gold turned to pale pink, then intensified, glowing brighter and brighter. Not just on the horizon, but in the air itself. She walked out onto the patio and took a deep breath, disappointed it didn't smell any different.

Her not-quite-awake-yet legs began to cramp in the cold. She thought about the hot, steaming cup she'd left behind, but didn't move, afraid to miss even one second of the show. Bright pink held for a while, but faded, little by little, to a pale coral. A slight breeze feathered the tinted fog, and it moved like stirred water. Pale coral to gold, and then, a hint of purple before it returned to a more familiar color, white with hints of gray. The faint round shape of a mist-smothered sun rose out of reach of the foothills. Shaylee caught herself thinking, 'I wish Jim could see this.'

It was a slow, stiff shuffle into the house. She closed the door and locked it, but hesitated, not quite ready to turn around. She knew what she would see when she did: an empty house, an empty day. He'd been gone almost three months, but her mind kept finding its way back to him. Moving on wasn't easy when there was no place to go.

¤ ¤ ¤ ¤ ¤ ¤ ¤ ¤ ¤ ¤ ¤ ¤ ¤

On the second Friday of December, Shaylee's publicist called.

"Hey, Babe. It's Sal," he announced in a gravelly, booming voice. She chuckled. There was no need for Salvatore Magestro to announce himself. He was immediately recognizable, over the phone or in person. Sal looked exactly the way he sounded: short, pudgy, balding, sweaty. He was all hyperactivity and bluster, personality traits that made him so good at his job.

"Look, darlin'. I'm not sure how to say this. I typed 'til my knuckles were blue and talked 'til my voice was hoarse." He paused to add a theatrical voice clearing. "I tried my darnedest to set up some public appearances for you, but, but . . .

"No one's interested," she finished for him.

"I don't understand it. I just, just don't," he said, sounding appropriately incensed. A short silence was followed by a tentative question. "You aren't disappointed, are you?"

"No," she promised him, "I'm not disappointed."

Relief was the emotion that came over her. The book itself proved how well she'd done her job. It was some of her best work. Shaylee knew it. The critics new it, and so did everyone who mattered. She didn't need the recognition, or a spotlight to bask in. That would be left up to Jim. James Vincent was the celebrity. He was the reason for the book, and, really, how many people looking at the night sky were interested in the darkness that held up the stars?

¤¤¤¤¤¤¤¤¤¤¤¤¤

On the last day of December, the first sales reports came in. Estimates had been in the 80,000 to 100,000 range. The verified number: 245,000 e-books and 120,000 paperbacks sold in forty-seven days.

¤¤¤¤¤¤¤¤¤¤¤¤¤

January didn't hold any surprises. When the Christmas and New Year's parties ended, the cycle of short, cold days and long cold nights was at its height. Fog and rain were the norms, with nothing new to look at in the forests. Gray day followed gray day, each about the same as the one before. The thermometer barely moved. Forty-one degrees during the day, thirty-eight overnight.

Shaylee's thoughts ran the same circles. Nothing realized. Nothing resolved. Just long hours that blended together and played over themselves. She didn't even feel inspired to cross any new books off of her reading list, finding herself drawn to favorite, familiar stories.

Watership Down, The Sunne In Splendor, Of Mice and Men, The Boy and The Otter, My Antonia, A Christmas Carol, Different Seasons, ...And Ladies Of The Club, Reindeer Moon, The Color Purple: characters she was comfortable with, places she'd visited before.

On the first Wednesday of February that cycle of rain was broken. The moisture-laden jet stream was pushed south by an Arctic airflow that dropped down from the North. The skies cleared. The sun shined. For six glorious days, her winter routine turned into a race against time, and weather. Overnight temperatures dipped into the teens. Daytime highs didn't reach thirty. During those nights, the cold captured fog mid-air and laid it out over the ground. Shaylee woke to find a thin and shimmering layer of ice covering every surface. Landscapes resembled grainy and fading photographs.

Silver thaw mornings and bright afternoons were all the inspiration she needed. Bundling up in layers of clothes, she grabbed her camera and drove, just drove.

Forests usually blurred by rain and pale mists were given new depth. Familiar scenery was reshaped by intense light and stark shadows. Sunlight reflected off melting ice to create light shows - flashes of color and crystal effects. At just the right angle, dewdrops turned into rainbows.

Those beautiful blue sky days kept her body busy with hiking and photography. They kept her mind busy with surveying, categorizing, cropping, and editing digital images. They kept her so engaged she had to remind herself what she was trying to do, forget about Jim. On the second Tuesday of February, the rains returned. So did the gray days. So did her gray mood. The rest of the month passed at an achingly slow pace.

How could such a short month feel so long? Why did winter feel more like a prison sentence than a season? She ran out of ways to wonder, 'When will it be over?' But that didn't stop her from thinking it, and saying it, and feeling it, for the next six weeks.

It was March Eighteenth, a Tuesday. At three thirty-one p.m., it reached *fifty-nine degrees*, the first not cold day of the year. She walked to the mailbox without wearing a coat, or a jacket, or a heavy sweater. It was a wonderful and freeing feeling.

Every season had its firsts, and, because she'd been looking for any hints of change, she was quick to see them. There they were, on the horizon; hazy chartreuse shadows. There they were, in the trees; catkins and tree buds, the beginnings of blossoms and leaves. There they were, on the ground; pale shoots of new grass and emerging seedlings that would soon become her summer field. All were turning points she'd been waiting for: Proof of Spring.

March was also a turning point for Jim's autobiography. The end of the month marked over 600,000 copies sold. Jim's absence only added to the already potent mystique that surrounded him. It fueled speculation. It fueled rumors. It fueled book sales. Tern Publishing took pre-orders for leather-bound, gilt-edged first edition hardbacks. The scheduled release date: June First. The number of copies: 350,000.

Winter asked nothing of Shaylee, but Spring begged for her attention. April began a growing riot. The wind blew one way and brought the rich aroma of lilacs. It blew another and with it came the delicate spice of apple blossoms. It changed direction again and carried the smell of warm grass. The wind that came out of the forest held the honey-sweet hints of tree pollens. If there was no wind, the sun and rising heat made a new perfume; a combination of them all.

She didn't think about apple blossoms for a whole year, until she walked under her Golden Delicious tree. Then, fragrance fell over her like a scented veil and it was all she could think about. She walked away, and then remembered something else. How it clung to her hair and clothes. How it followed her into the house, the ghost of a perfume that didn't last long, one she would need to go outside to reapply.

The last week of April. Jim was six months gone, and Shaylee still thought about him too much. Yes, he was one of the most handsome men in the world. Yes, he'd shared his most intimate secret with her, and, yes, he had fulfilled a fantasy, or two. All were good reasons (excuses?) to keep their time together fresh in her mind.

The sights, the sounds, the mood of his first experience. Her skin remembered his touch. Her ears remembered his moans. They made love four times before the sun went down on that day. Just the thought of it brought tingling, tightening sensations to . . . several parts of her body.

Was all of her pain worth that? First, she smiled. Then, she laughed under her breath. 'Yes.' The answer to that question was, and always would be, 'Yes.'

May Fourteenth. There were only ten days until her forty-fifth birthday, and she was still trying to find a way to get on with her life. A trip around the property with a bowl to collect tea makings brought a moment of clarity. While plucking fir needles from a low branch, Jim came to her mind. She steeled herself for the pain, but it didn't come. The memory came to her alone.

Yes. It was happening. The pain was beginning to separate itself from the memories. Could it be possible? That she could think out, not just feel, her experiences with Jim.

During a cup of fresh rose petal and cinnamon tea, an idea came to her. Take a daily drive, somewhere out into the country, maybe two hours out and two hours back. During those drives, she could think about Jim all she wanted. Then, when the drive was finished, so were her thoughts about Jim.

Day One:

Shaylee thought about the Mitchell Quinn story. Had her instincts compelled her to share it with Jim? Mitch had manipulated their meeting. He'd used his family and friends to deceive her into a smoke-and-mirrors relationship. From the beginning of his carefully orchestrated ruse, he'd known how deeply he would hurt her.

Had Jim done the same? Interviews and internet biographies turned her life story into public knowledge. They all made it clear that she was unattached, available, and open to any and all new experiences. It was possible he'd researched that information, and then, once he'd met her, decided she could be the one to help him. Was it a convenient coincidence he'd chosen an attractive, single woman to be his biographer?

She thought back to the day she finished Jim's accident chapter, to his reactions after he read it. On that evening, his attitude towards her changed. He began to look at her differently, and, to act differently towards her. He might not have had any ulterior motives. It was possible he'd found in her words not only a story, but evidence of her compassion and understanding. It could have been a defining moment for him. One that spurred him into thought. And, when the opportunity presented itself, into action.

She sent her mind even further back, to their first meeting, to his white-knuckled grip on the doorknob. The reason he'd given her for his nervousness was a fear of sharing his private life with the public. It had, even then, seemed a little out of proportion with his behavior. She tried to remember the way he'd looked at her, his tone of voice, the things he'd said, the things he hadn't said. Was his obvious anxiety on that day its own answer?

At least, with Jim, she'd known what she was walking into. With Jim, she'd known just how far to let her heart wander. She could have refused his request. She could have refused him, but clearly saw an adventure in his eyes, and, willingly followed it.

When he approached her, when he offered himself to her, they both knew it wasn't love. It was a lifeline, a desperate attempt to face and conquer fear. It was intense, and it was emotional, but it wasn't love. When he left, when his plans led him to move on, it wasn't hate. It was something they both knew was going to happen. It was leaving. It was change, and it was loss, but it wasn't hate.

Day Two:

The toy boat armada was something else that kept coming into her mind. It was a surprise event, an unexpected experience that turned into a beautiful memory. But no matter how beautiful, or perfect, it was meant to be only occasionally visited and enjoyed. It was never meant to be a permanent place of residence.

She did think about Jim a little less. Sometimes, he wasn't the first thing she thought about in the morning. Sometimes, he wasn't her last thought before falling asleep. But that had more to do with the passing of time than the setting of limits.

Maybe, she needed to stop trying anything. Loss was a process, not a scheduled event. Maybe, she should accept the memories and emotions that found her, just let them come and go. Her mind was telling her what to do, but those instructions were in direct conflict with her feelings. Maybe her brain needed to be reminded that the soul has its own plans.

Day Three:

She couldn't stop herself from seeing their relationship as a puzzle in need of solving. What had Jim taken away from their time together? Why couldn't she stop thinking about all he'd given her?

Then, there was something from inside of her that was missing. Why couldn't she figure out what it was? And, what about the part of Jim that had stayed behind? It was something she could feel every time she thought about him. Why couldn't she pinpoint it, or give it a name?

Was she trying to solve a problem that couldn't be solved? Had she been asking questions that didn't have answers? Was it that easy, that she'd simply been faced with a truth, and all she needed to do was accept it?


Day Four:

Country drives were meant to be spontaneous fun, not painstaking chores. She needed to approach her situation the way she did her drives. Don't try to plan or arrange them, just surrender to whatever might happen. She'd been putting too much pressure on herself and needed to stop. Time to go with the flow. Working through Jim would take as long as it took. No shortcuts. No cheating. No speed-healing.


Shaylee pulled over to a small roadside waterfall fed by the melting snowpack of Mount Saint Helens. Water poured over the rocks with crisp slapping sounds. Memories of thirst told her the water would be cold and clean. She approached it with cupped hands that filled quickly. The water was cold, and clean, and sweet with the spice of spring. The last of it spilled through her fingers, landed at her feet, and disappeared into the grass.

On the drive home, the road felt like it was carrying her along, not just holding her up.

¤ ¤ ¤ ¤ ¤ ¤ ¤ ¤ ¤ ¤ ¤ ¤ ¤ ¤

Eight months had passed. In that time, her pain had eased. Her fears had calmed. Out of control thoughts were manageable again. She'd put off using her strongest healing tool, writing, not ready to face the raw emotions inspired by Jim. But maybe, just maybe, it was time.

Sitting down at the computer felt wrong. It wasn't personal. It wasn't spontaneous. She knew what she needed. To her bedroom. To her nightstand. To the waiting stack of spiral-bound notebooks inside its top drawer. The notebook with her ideas for Jim's poem lay on top. She set it aside, a project for another time. It would be a summary of her feelings for Jim, and that day was still a long way off.

Armed with full pens and empty pages, she wrote about their first phone call and went from there. She wrote everything she remembered, and she remembered everything. The details playing hide-and-seek inside her head escaped into ink and onto paper. Tears found the pages. Laughter found them too. The notebooks filled with stories, with emotions, with memories. They filled with Jim. It felt good and bad. It felt frightening and freeing. It felt coming and going, but, most of all, it felt right.

There was no rush to the writing. Inspiration came in soft waves, the same way heat rose gently and gradually fell over the course of the day. Skies were blue. Winds were calm. The rest of May came and went. June passed the same way, mellow and quiet. During her walks, she kept an eye on the wildflowers; which ones were blooming, which ones were fading, and which ones were dying.

Notebook number five was opened on the morning of July Second. She took it out onto the deck and sat down with it at the table. As she titled and numbered it, she thought of a grassy hill down the road. The hill itself was part of a neighboring valley. A year-round creek ran below it and another hillside rose above it to the East. To the North and South were forests. The grass would be about up to her knees, a good wading height.

The notebook, some pens, a bottled water, and a packet of trail mix went into a long-strapped hiking bag. The strap went around her neck and over her right shoulder. The pouch settled under her left arm, in the curve of her waist.

At the end of the driveway, she headed east for about five minutes. It led towards a bend in the road. There, she came to an abrupt stop. The green grasses, white daisies, blue bachelor buttons, and pink clover were all gone. They'd been chopped down, piled into neat rows, and left to dry. A sinking feeling found her, disappointment hinting at loss, but it didn't last long. A slight breeze came towards her, and with it, the smell of fresh-cut hay.

Sweet was a blanket description, one she'd used before. But the distinct scent was more than that. It was the memory of all her summers. It was the essence of nature itself: rain mixed with sun mixed with air mixed with time. In a few days, farm equipment would transform it into bales, load it up, and truck it all away. Left behind would be stubble covered earth. It would appear barren, but not for long. The field would be stimulated by the rains. It would be revived by the sun. The grasses' roots would send out new stalks. Those stalks would grow tall and straight, but would yield to make room for wildflowers. Soon enough, the field would regrow, with no memory it had ever been mown.

A lone coyote trotted across the road at the bottom of the hill. A mated pair of Gyrfalcons circled over their trimmed hunting grounds. Confused bees searched for missing flowers. They all found Shaylee at the edge of the field, writing in her notebook.


On July Tenth, her own publisher checked in on her. "It's been over six months," Jiney kindly reminded her in an e-mail message. "Are you thinking about your next novel?"

Jinette Ashley Winstead-Stormme was the mother of four, grandmother of nine, and great-grandmother of two. Her fashion statement was a vast collection of brightly flowered calf-length dresses. All were cinched around her thickening waist with wide leather belts. Long, silver-gray hair neatly circled the top of her head in a thick, braided bun. It was a fitting, no-nonsense look for a down-to-earth woman.

The family pictures in Jiney's office documented her aging. She'd been born with rich auburn hair that had mellowed and faded over the years. Though she'd never volunteered her age, Shaylee was sure she was at least sixty-five.

Jiney was a strong woman with a quiet dignity, and Shaylee had liked her from the instant they met. It wasn't because Jiney had only good things to say about her writing. It was because she could tell Jiney meant what she said. She later learned her first instincts were right. Straight talk without flattery was how Jiney communicated. If she didn't like something, she said nothing. If she did, she couldn't say enough.

Four larger publishing houses had approached her. They all offered condescending attitudes and restrictive contracts. Jiney's approach had been sweetly different. She wrote Shaylee a charming, hand written letter after reading "Some Of Me." In the letter, she introduced herself, complimented the story, and offered Shaylee a book-by-book contract.

Shaylee penned her own hand written letter in reply. Phone calls were exchanged and a meeting was set. It was a wonderful excuse to visit New York City, and it was the beginning of a lucrative alliance.

Her responding e-mail was simple and clear, something Jiney would appreciate. "There are some personal things I need to sort through. I'm going to need at least the rest of the summer. Maybe a little longer."

Jiney's reply was a list of recommended summer reading, all new novels by known authors. Below that, a single sentence: "If you're not going to write, you should at least be checking up on the competition."

'Maybe when I'm done with this,' she thought as she picked up a partially filled notebook, notebook number six. 'I've got some beautiful demons to excise first.

## The Last Chapter

September Fourth. It was a year, to the day, that Jim left her house, and, it was the day he'd chosen for his return to Hollywood.

Shaylee was baking bread and half-listening to the news. *"While in the United Kingdom, he underwent a series of experimental nerve grafting surgeries. Thankfully, those procedures were successful. Mr. Vincent is again 'fully functional.' He was able to juggle the procedures with his film schedule. In a press release statement, he expressed his gratitude to his surgeons. He was thankful for the patience and support of his film crew, his producers, his fellow actors . . ."*

"No. No. No. No. No. No. No." The denial song flowed from her as she rushed through the kitchen towards the television. Even what little she heard was too much. A copy of the statement, thoughtfully forwarded by Sal, found its way onto the fire. Tern Publishing's news release e-mail was ceremoniously deleted. Two bullets dodged only to be blind-sided by a sniper - the local news. As the screen went dark, Shaylee shook her head. One more defeat in the game she'd invented: 'Avoid The Jim.'

The rules were simple. Walk past newsstands without stopping. Look at the floor and only the floor until the cash register was reached at check-out stands. Magazine isles in the markets were off-limits. No book stores. Channel surf past all national news, talk shows, and celebrity gossip spots.

It wasn't an easy game to win. Pictures, headlines, his whereabouts, his plans - there was no avoiding them. They were splashed across every newspaper, every magazine, every tabloid, everywhere. Sometimes, she couldn't walk away, or look away, fast enough. Sometimes her channel surfing timing was off.

And the computer? There were so many James Vincent media bombs going off it felt like a war zone. Any e-mails with his name in the title or subject line were erased, but it didn't help much. Most website home pages had their own news feeds, and in the blink of an eye, another point was lost.

It was by information osmosis that she knew Jim was making the rounds on the talk show circuit. Daytime, late-night, network, and cable. That he was seen at a Hollywood party in the company of a petite young starlet. That two weeks later he went on a Rodeo Drive shopping spree with a South African supermodel. None of those sightings upset her as much as finding out he attended a D.C. charity gala. At the White House. Personally invited by the President Of The United States.

¤ ¤ ¤ ¤ ¤ ¤ ¤ ¤ ¤ ¤ ¤ ¤ ¤ ¤

Somewhere among writing and breathing, eating and sleeping, thinking and crying, laughing and remembering, three months went by. September became October. October found its way to November, and November knew the way to December. Time passed, but nothing changed. Shaylee was stuck in an invisible trap that wouldn't let her go. Jim's first tentative touch. Jim's last kiss. A few short weeks of her life that felt like her whole world.

Holiday celebrations brought with them a familiar and welcome set of routines. They would have guided her gently to the end of the year, if not for one thing: Jim's independent film. It was set for release on Christmas day. Christmas day.

Shaylee didn't think it was possible for anything to ruin her favorite time of year. David had tried a few times, but couldn't succeed. Jim had actually done it, whether he'd intended to or not.

She couldn't listen to radio Christmas music. She couldn't watch her favorite live broadcast holiday specials. All were peppered with promotions for James Vincent's new movie, "We Watch The Rising Stars." Every television commercial, every radio ad, every errant flyer stole a little bit of her joy.

It was no use. She couldn't fight it anymore. December 26th and she was at Vancouver Mall. Past the after-Christmas sales. Past the food court. Past the new coffee shop she'd been dying to visit. The theater was ahead, around the corner. Her pace slowed, but she didn't stop. The theater alcove came into view and she froze mid-step. Her right foot instantly dropped, but her left foot needed help finding the floor. Then, a pause in time, while her brain told her what her eyes were seeing.

In front of her, inside the theater lobby's glass doors, was a life-sized cut-out of Jim. It was poor quality, and the eyes were looking up and away, but it felt as though she'd just met up with James Vincent.

In the moments she looked at 'him,' his grainy face, his insincere smile, his averted eyes, a judgment was made. There was no such thing as a classy cardboard cut-out. Then, a decision was made. She walked past 'him' and into the theater. The cardboard Jim was afraid to look at her, but she wasn't afraid of him. Inside that theater was her own doubt, her own past, her own pain, and it was time to stare them all down.

Would it help? Hard to tell. Would it show her the way out of the rut she'd been in?

"Maybe," she whispered. A big tub of popcorn and a lot of apprehension escorted her into the screening room.


As she walked out of the theater, Shaylee smiled. She smiled to the cardboard cut-out of Jim. She looked south and smiled to the real Jim, where ever he might be. His acting had taken on a new confidence, a new strength. On that screen, in his performance, was something unmistakable. It was something she was, in part, responsible for.

She smiled to the people she passed. She smiled to the parking lot, and then, to her rear-view mirror. In one of the scenes, Jim gave a speech of thanks. When he spoke the words, 'because of you,' he looked deliberately into the camera. The shot froze, and he held the gaze for several seconds. She knew the expression. She recognized the tone of voice. The words, and their message, were meant for her; a private moment shared with the public. It was a sweet bit of irony. It was Jim's sense of humor. In the scene was also his confession, one he might never make in person.

It must have been the catalyst, the one missing piece needed to turn an ending into a beginning. A calm came over her, a calm that was hard to describe because it was like nothing she'd felt before. What happened next was what she'd been waiting for, but it still came as a gentle surprise: acceptance.

She took a deep breath and her lungs filled with that acceptance. She exhaled, and it spilled out to surround her. She didn't walk through the door, she glided. The evening flowed around her, offering no resistance. Her thoughts were light, but her eyelids were heavy. Anticipation for the coming day settled into bed with her, but she easily fell into a deep sleep.

The morning was cold and quiet, but not her mind. In her mind, memories of Jim were stirring, moving, pleading to be noticed. Overnight, they'd changed, and they wanted to show her how they'd changed. Red hot emotions had mellowed to cool orange. Rough edges had smoothed to soft lines. Loud screams had quieted to hushed undertones. They were still inside her. They were all still inside her, but they were no longer at war with her, and she didn't feel any need to do battle with them.

The following days were each new miracles in their own right. She was finally able to celebrate that Jim had happened. She was finally able to remember it all without pain. The meeting that became a collaboration. The collaboration that became a friendship. The friendship that became a romance. The romance that became an ending.

She knew there were some moments Jim would always remember. She knew there were some things she might try to forget. She knew that, sometimes, she would smile, and that Jim would be the reason for her smile. She knew that sometimes, tears would come to her eyes, Jim, the reason behind them.

She also knew that one day he would be reading this.

Shaylee sat down at her computer, a stack of twelve neatly labeled notebooks on the desk beside her. On top was ~Jim ~ One. She opened it.

"Yes," the word came out as a whisper.

A crooked half-smile came to her face, a bit of private laughter behind it. Her next words were strong, confident.

"Yes, this is going to make one very interesting story."

## ~ End ~

**Closure**

Shaylee stopped and started many times. She obsessively poured over it, and then completely ignored it. She told herself to just forget about it, and then returned to it with apologies for having been away so long. When, finally, Jim's poem was complete, she carefully copied it into her poetry notebook.

# A Poem

What did it mean to you

when you gave me your secrets,

and I found a place for them

in a carved wooden box

with my dried flowers and prayers?

What did it mean to you

when I claimed the silence between us

and we discovered

that the story's ending

was its beginning as well?

What did it mean to you

when I stole the fear from your eyes,

when we followed the ocean to each other,

the stars our only light,

the sand our only bed,

the waves our only music?

What did it mean to you?

What did I mean to you?

## A Letter To "Mitchell Quinn"

It was a hot day, a day like many I experienced living in Philadelphia. The sun went down, but the heat remained. The humidity was thick, and the mood on that evening was even thicker, because I was ending our relationship. I don't remember anything I said, and I probably ever will, just the noise of myself mumbling a few weak, breathless words. I don't remember you leaving my home. I don't remember crying that night, but I'm sure I did. I might even have cried all night. But, I do remember what came next: a hundred different kinds of pain, and having to live through them all, one by one.

Being in love was . . . it was never touching the ground. It was secret smiles in public places. It was my brain and body in amazing harmony, like the high of listening to a favorite song all. the. time. It gave me the strength and confidence to claim my place in the world. Where ever I was, that was where I was meant to be. I didn't have all the answers, and it didn't matter. I didn't have wealth or fame, but I didn't care. I had one thing, one very important thing. Love. I wore it proudly, every moment of every day. It became everything I was. It gave my life a flavor I'd never tasted before. It fueled a pure kind of joy I'd never known before.

Letting you go meant letting go of that too. It was so hard to feel it separating itself from me, but I couldn't stop it. Little by little, day by day, insight by insight, it pulled away. It had been so inter-twined with me, it took pieces of me away with it. That love's gradual abandonment didn't simply leave empty holes where it had been. Every corresponding bit of it was replaced with an equal amount of pain. I can only be grateful it didn't happen all at once.

I went into a subtle and cushioned kind of shock. I was able to function. I woke. I moved. I ate, and worked, and walked, and slept, but everything around me was disjointed and hazy. People walked into within an arms length and I could see them, hear them, touch them, but as soon as they walked away, they disappeared into a muffled and blurry no-man's-land. The only distinction between days were my memories of you, and the types and amounts of pain they brought. When the daze lifted, I was one year older, and forever changed.

'Write about what hurt you.' - a good piece of advice. Until I penned the story of us, I thought I'd completely healed, but once I started writing, I learned differently. I began early one morning and didn't leave the computer until the sun went down. The whole time, I was shaking. When I re-read what I'd written the next day, I was shaking. At some point during the first re-write, I stopped shaking, and as I read it through the third time, I felt relief, an awkward kind of relief. There it was, an embarrassment that was finally out of me and into words, actual words. Every event, in order. Every emotion, if not named, was at least place-marked so I could return to it whenever I wanted or needed to. A tangible story. It was painful, and it was tragic, but it was mine. There was an uncomfortable comfort in knowing it existed.

As I rewrote and edited it over the next few days, I also found myself facing a difficult fact. What had happened between us, or, more accurately, what you'd done to me, was an ordeal I would never truly 'get over.' How do you get over such a betrayal from the love of your life? How do you get over having to change every dream you'd ever had? The simple answer is, 'You don't.' I'd gone through too much. I'd lost too much. I'd been hurt so deeply and scarred so completely that I had no choice but to accept my memories of you as permanent residents. It was a conflict with denial and acceptance that created those demons. But when I started to call them by name, when I set a place for them at my table, I finally knew peace.

There still remain unanswered questions that I can't stop myself from asking – a few lingering wounds that refuse to scar over – a random ache for something missing – the echoing emptiness of an unlived life. Once in a while I even catch myself thinking that if you'd understood my dreams, if you'd seen how beautiful they were, you wouldn't just have wanted to be a part of them, you would have done everything in your power to bring them true. But then, I remembered. I remembered what I was to you, and it was nothing like what you were to me.

The first time I saw you after our break up, the song "In The Air Tonight" played in my head. You drove up in a black Jaguar. You stepped out of it in a black tuxedo. You walked up to me with a big smile. You wanted only one thing. On that day, I *felt* the meaning of that haunting song. It captured the essence of seeing someone from your past and realizing that you never really knew them. On that day came a flood of stark, brutal understanding. The time we'd spent together, the intimacies we'd shared, the love I'd given you, it had all been spent on a mere visitor to my world. As I watched you drive away, it hit me like a velvet hammer. I'd lived five years of my life in the lies of a stranger.

Only you know the parts I left out, and, they were left out for a reason. Writing is about facing emotions, experiencing emotions, expressing emotions. It's about laying them out in front of you and seeing them look back at you. The omitted parts are personal battles I need to save for another time. One day, the whole story, every part of it, will come out of me. One day, I will be able to face those mistakes, those imperfections, those demons, those shames. Just not today.

So - what did I learn from you? I learned that I could force myself to walk away from even the most precious things in my life. I learned that I could walk away from *anything*.

I think the saddest part of it all is that I don't associate you with anything wonderful, special, or beautiful in my life. All the best is gone. This acknowledgement started with the death of our relationship because I only clearly remember the pain, the sorrow, and the crushing emotions of an ending. When I think of you, I'm forever leaving.

I want no new memories of you, but if I could ask one question it would be: What story would you write about me?

End Note:

"Mitchell" died suddenly in 2014, at the age of 62. Every time I think about that, I smile. Not a vindictive smile, not an angry smile, just a smile of relief that he can't hurt anyone anymore.

## Author's Notes

1). What I learned about writing a novel I learned by writing ~Jim~. The first draft took me two weeks of straight typing, sunrise-to-sunset typing. It looked like something I would have written as a teenager, and it sucked. But it was written, finally written; the first draft of my first novel.

When I read it again, I saw in front of me ideas that had been churning in the background, ideas I'd given permission to escape onto a page. I took a middle-heavy story and all of those ideas to the next level: cohesion. I expanded them one by one. My second draft was better. Nothing to brag about, but better. With the third draft laid out in front of me, I clearly saw what was missing: "The Mood."

"The Mood" was my driving force from that time on. "The Mood" challenged me and encouraged me. It turned ~Jim~ into literature, and me into a novelist.

During that process, it became its own destination. The emotions down on paper, I could conjure, remember, experience them all in a safe and controlled arena. I don't know how many tears I cried, but they were tears of progress, not desperation. Everything I wrote had been a part of me long before it was named and documented. It was discovery as well as creativity. In the process, during the progress, I learned about myself. It was a priceless gift, one I am grateful for every day.

So it is here that I say thank you to myself. I too was a work in progress. I too was disjointed ideas brought together. I'd always dreamed of a butterfly rebirth: completely shedding my past, emerging new, perfect and beautiful from a discarded shell. But that isn't what happens to the butterfly. Its caterpillar body adapts tools for a different existence. The same brain, the same eyes; but longer legs for grace, a gentler mouth for delicate sipping, light and flexible appendages to carry it. Not new, but a mix of earthbound past and winged future. And that's what I did. I used my past to make a womb. I chose my own birthplace. And, after my long sleep ended, I emerged; the humble bones of my past supporting the fanciful wings of my future.

2) When writing, I don't like to be distracted by typing numbers, so one thing you might have noticed is that almost every number in my story is spelled out. The other reason: I have never been fond of math. Well, 'not

fond' isn't quite accurate. How much I love the English language is equally proportionate to how much I hate math. So, turning numbers into words is a sweet and personal revenge for me. I am smiling as I read this paragraph.

3) Here is where I name-drop. Everyone is related to someone famous, and my lauded relative is William Sidney Porter, also known as O. Henry. He is a relative of my deceased maternal grandfather, Raymond Bryan Porter. I am NOT related to any of the already famous Baldwins - piano makers, writers, actor brothers . . .

4) Shaylee's adventures will continue. I'm also working several novels of inter-related short stories (my shout out to "Different Seasons"). There are many works-in-progress waiting patiently in my computer. It will be a toss-up as to which I finish and publish first.

5) One of the hardest things about writing this story was finishing it. It was an idea I gave birth to, then helped to grow from a simple idea to a full story. It was a friend, inviting me to visit and to create. It was a confidant I was always sad to leave. Once I declared it complete, I knew I would never be able to return to it in the same way. It changed from a work-in-progress, mentally challenging me to do what I could, to a finished project, showing me what I'd done. And, learned yet another way to say good-bye.

6) I have a private Facebook group for ~Jim~. Please send me a private message for an invitation. I am the lyricist of an online musical group: Beyond Atlantic. That Facebook page is public. I am also on Pinterest. My boards are a voluminous collection of my varied interests.

7) And, lastly, I ask that you PLEASE, PLEASE, PLEASE be careful when sharing the details of this story with anyone who has not yet read it. I don't know how many times I've had the endings of books and movies unintentionally ruined by well-meaning people who just wanted to share their enthusiasm, but accidentally ruined plot twists or endings.

Thank you.

# Webography

https://www.merckmanuals.com/professional/neurologic-disorders/coma-and-impaired-consciousness/vegetative-state-and-minimally-conscious-state

https://www.cdc.gov/heartdisease/atrial_fibrillation.htm

https://www.history.com/topics/vietnam-war/vietnam-war-timeline

https://aquarium.org/visit/hours/

http://bugguide.net/node/view/7997:  Metallic Green Bee - Genus Agapostemon - Metallic Green Bees. ... (2003) Phylogeny of the bee genus Agapostemon (Hymenoptera: Halictidae). Systematic Entomology 28(1): 101–124.

http://journalistsresource.org:
Chicago Manual of Style basics - Journalist's Resource

https://cooktoria.com/sweet-crepes/

http://garden.org/learn/articles/view/2102/:  National Gardening Association:  Rose of Sharon bush is a deciduous flowering shrub, sometimes thought of as a small tree. Learn about pruning it and other growing tips here.

http://www.ireland-information.com/heraldichall/irishsurnames.htm

http://www.mountsthelens.com/images/map-504-cc.jpg

http://philadelphiaencyclopedia.org

http://philadelphianeighborhoods.com

https://www.radiocab.net/#/booking/

https://www.thebalancecareers.com/hospitality-job-titles-2061496

http://www.visitphilly.com/philadelphia-neighborhoods/#sm.00000yhc5xxh5jdv4wumwz5qd8ed5

https://en.wikipedia.org/wiki/Chinook_Winds_Casino

https://en.wikipedia.org/wiki/Fibromyalgia

https://en.wikipedia.org/wiki/Glossary_of_French_expressions_in_English

https://en.wikipedia.org/wiki/Papercrete

https://en.wikipedia.org/wiki/Sun_path#/media/File:Sun-path-polar-chart.svg: The sun's winter path:

https://www.almanac.com/plant/black-eyed-susans

Autumn Equinox 2014 - September 22:
https://www.nationalgeographic.com/science/article/1409022-first-day-of-fall-science-sun-space-autumnal-equinox#:~:text=Say%20goodbye%20to%20summer%3A%20The,a%20favorite%20season%20for%20many.

Exits from I-5:
https://en.wikipedia.org/wiki/Interstate_5_in_Washington

|   |   | 0.00 | 0.00 | Interstate Bridge — I-5 continues south into Oregon towards Portland |   |   |
|---|---|---|---|---|---|---|
| Clark | Vancouver | 0.41 | 0.66 | 1A | SR 14 east – Camas |   |
|   |   | 0.45 | 0.72 | 1B | 6th Street – Vancouver City Center | Northbound exit and southbound entrance |
|   |   | 1.05 | 1.69 | 1C | SR 501 (Mill Plain Boulevard) – Vancouver City Center, Port of Vancouver |   |

|   |   |   |   |   |   |   |
|---|---|---|---|---|---|---|
|   |   | 1.58 | 2.54 | 1D | 4th Plain Boulevard |   |
|   |   | 2.35 | 3.78 | 2 | SR 500 east / 39th Street |   |
|   |   | 3.07 | 4.94 | 3 | Northeast Highway 99, Main Street |   |
|   |   | 4.36 | 7.02 | 4 | Northeast 78th Street |   |
|   |   | 5.39 | 8.67 | 5 | Northeast 99th Street |   |
|   |   | 7.24 | 11.65 | 7A | Northeast 134th Street | Northbound exit and southbound entrance; southbound exit is via I-205 |
|   |   |   |   | 7B | Northeast 139th Street | No southbound exit |
|   |   | 7.48 | 12.04 | 7 | I-205 south / Northeast 134th Street – Salem | Southbound exit and northbound entrance |
|   |   | 9.51 | 15.30 | 9 | Northeast 179th Street – Clark County Fairgrounds |   |
|   |   | 11.20 | 18.02 | 11 | SR 502 east (Northeast 219th Street) – Battle Ground |   |
|   | Ridgefield | 14.21 | 22.87 | 14 | SR 501 west (Pioneer Street) – Ridgefield |   |
|   |   | 16.80 | 27.04 | 16 | Northwest La Center Road – La Center |   |

| Cowlitz | Woodland | 21.08 | 33.92 | 21 | SR 503 east – Woodland, Cougar | |
| | | 22.72 | 36.56 | 22 | Dike Access Road | |
| | | 27.70 | 44.58 | 27 | Todd Road – Port of Kalama | |
| | Kalama | 29.84 – 30.64 | 48.02 – 49.31 | 30 | Kalama | |

# ~Jim~ Special Fonts - Freeware

Cover Picture:
Blurb: Banksia - (fonts2u)
~Jim~: jr!hand (fonts2u.com)
by Suzann Baldwin: Inconsolata (fontsquirrel.com)

Cover Blurb, Table of Contents and A Dedication To Healing:

Banksia - (fonts2u)


Shaylee's Handwriting:
**Dawning Of A New Day** - bold (fonts2u.com)

Jim's Handwriting:
jr!hand (fonts2u.com)

Porterhouse steak stamp:
**Boston Traffic - (Fontsquirrel.com**

The Story:
Inconsolata (fontsquirrel.com)

Attorney Name/Legal Complaint Heading:
LibreBaskerville (fontsquirrel.com)

Attorney's Letter:
**LM Roman 10 (fonts2u.com)**

Harold Mayhew-Reese name and title:
Diplomata - (fontsquirrel.com)

Copyright 2025 by Suzann Baldwin. All Rights Reserved.